Olympu

Costumes
& Copiers

Book Three

Kelly Pawlik

For permission, please email
olympicvistapublishing@gmail.com
Website: olympicvistapublishing.com

Bookstores and wholesale orders can be placed through
olympicvistapublishing@gmail.com

Cover art design: Greta Paliulyte

Pawlik, Kelly, author
Issued in print and electronic formats
ISBN 978-1-7777181-5-2 (paperback)
ISBN 978-1-7777181-6-9 (epub)

DISCLAIMER
This is a work of fiction. Any names and characters are used fictitiously or are the product of the author's imagination. Any resemblance to actual persons, living or dead, is entirely coincidental.

OLYMPIC VISTA
PUBLISHING

This book is dedicated
to Adelaide and Darius.
You may not be flesh and bone,
but my adventures with you are real.

Part One

One

The trees had turned from green to a panoply of yellow, orange, and red. The crisp autumn air licked at Adelaide's cheeks as she stepped out of her house. She smiled at the grey sky. It looked like it would rain.

"You could smile at me, you know," Tetsu said. His dark hair protruded from his head like the bristles of a hedgehog. He wore pressed khakis and a polo shirt, a uniform enforced by his mother, much to his dismay. "I don't know why you're smiling at the clouds. It isn't like we don't see them every day."

"I like the rain." Adelaide pulled the door closed behind her and locked it. Tetsu knocked on her door every weekday morning, except for a brief period earlier this school year when she'd been mad at him. The day didn't feel right if he wasn't here, but she wasn't about to admit that. Tetsu's ego was big enough already. "And I see you every day, too," Adelaide added as she tucked the key into her bag. The two of them set off down the front steps.

"I'm way more charming than the rain. But if you like it, then you live in the right place," Tetsu grumbled.

Olympic Vista received even more rain than its neighbouring towns in Washington State did. Adelaide wondered if it had something to do with The Link, the research and development facility the town was built up around. She had given little thought to the weather or the facility until Darius had moved to town. His presence made her question everything.

"So, how was the date?" Tetsu asked.

She and Darius had gone to The Blue last night. It was an ancient theatre that played classic movies. The seats were an array of two-person benches and uncomfortable fold-down chairs. The two of them had managed to get one of the coveted benches. They had shared popcorn, and when the bag was empty, Darius held her hand. She liked how his hand felt wrapped around hers. His dad picked them up afterward and, sitting in the backseat, Darius had grinned at her the entire drive back to her house. He'd even walked her from the car to her front door.

"It was a movie." Adelaide stared straight ahead as they left her driveway and walked from the end of the dead-end road toward the bus stop.

"Come on, it was a date."

Adelaide didn't respond. Out of the corner of her eye, she noticed the door of her next-door-neighbour's house open.

Tetsu shuddered and focused on the end of the road as Adelaide's neighbour, Mr. Fudder, stepped out of his house. He was an older man with thin white hair and a clean-shaven face. He was stooped with a slight paunch and was always dressed in a cardigan. Today's cardigan was dark blue.

Adelaide waved and Mr. Fudder waved back.

"Don't do that," Tetsu hissed.

"Why not? He's just a person."

"You don't know that. There's something wrong with him. Like, Link wrong." His voice was urgent, desperate. He quickened his pace and led them down the street.

"That's ridiculous." Adelaide knew Tetsu was secretly terrified of Mr. Fudder. He was strange, to be sure, but Adelaide wasn't convinced he posed a threat to anyone.

Kurt slipped out of his front door and hurried down the walkway. Despite his short stature and scrawny build, Kurt's pants were a pinch too short and Adelaide

5

could see the tops of his socks. Kurt brushed his reddish-brown hair away from his eyes as he fell in step with Tetsu and Adelaide. Then the three of them stopped in front of the house next door.

"Well," Tetsu said, "someone should go get her." He gestured toward the two-storey house. The green grass was trimmed short and the garden bloomed with purple geraniums.

"She'll be out in a minute," Adelaide said. Sophie had been less kind to them since they all transitioned to their last year of elementary school. While she endeavoured to get along with Sophie, she knew Sophie's older brother, Andy, was already on his own bus to the high school so there was no chance of seeing him.

As if on cue, Sophie emerged from the house. She had never been the most punctual of the friends, and her newfound love of makeup had exacerbated her tardiness.

"Oh good! You waited this time," Sophie said. Her long honey-blond locks had been coiffed to perfection. Today she wore bright pink pants with a matching rainbow stripped shirt just visible under her coat.

"Didn't seem to have a lot of choice," Tetsu said. "You made a show about it the other day."

"Whatever. So, how was your date?" Sophie asked

Adelaide. For a time, Sophie seemed to have her own crush on Darius, but Adelaide suspected it was his family's money and his status as the new, mysterious guy that had actually prompted her interest.

"She says it was a movie," Tetsu offered.

"It was a movie," Adelaide confirmed.

"Oh, come on, we all know you want to be his girlfriend," Sophie retorted.

Adelaide felt her cheeks flush.

"Right?" Tetsu asked.

"It would mean Andy leaves us alone," Sophie said.

Adelaide felt her cheeks redden even further at the mention of Sophie's brother. She wanted to ask what Sophie meant by her comment, but she didn't want to draw any more attention to herself.

"I finished *The Hitchhiker's Guide to the Galaxy* last night." Kurt gave Adelaide a small smile as he changed the subject. "The worst part of a book is the end."

"What?" Tetsu asked, confused.

"The end. It's the worst. You've become attached to these characters and then that's it. You won't see them do anything else."

"That's so lame. I cannot believe you have a girlfriend and I don't. And Farrah?" Tetsu kicked a stray rock into the ditch. "It doesn't make sense."

Farrah, Kurt's long-time crush, was one of the most popular girls at the school. She had big blond hair and a gaggle of girlfriends. It had shocked everyone when she'd started to date Kurt. Adelaide attributed Kurt's sudden surge in popularity to Darius' sister Davia's interest in him. She knew Davia had feigned her interest, but the other girls didn't seem to have noticed. Farrah now thought she was lucky Kurt had chosen her over anyone else.

"Be nice, Tetsu," Adelaide said.

"I apologize," Tetsu said in an exaggerated fashion. "How *is* it going with your girlfriend, Kurt?"

"Good. Great?" Kurt sounded uncertain.

"Pathetic." Tetsu shook his head.

"Adelaide, how's your mom's job going?" Kurt asked, changing the subject once more.

"Good, actually," she replied.

"That's great!" Kurt said.

Her mother, Belinda, was notorious for her inability to keep a job. It had taken several weeks after being laid off from Bootlegger for her to secure a position with the copy centre in the mall. Belinda was proud of her new employment and delighted in wearing blouses, skirts, and heels to work. Adelaide insisted she be the one to iron them, fearful her mother would get distracted as she had in times past. Her mother was as skilled at burning clothing as she was at burning food. The domestic life just didn't suit her.

"That means an extra serving of sugary cereal this weekend," Tetsu said as he rubbed his hands together.

***

A shiny black Lincoln Town Car pulled into a parking stall outside James Morrison Elementary School.

"Darius, your mother will pick you up after school. I have to meet clients. Davia, I will be back in time to get you after practice," Drew Belcouer instructed his children. "Don't make me wait."

"Okay, Dad," Darius replied as he climbed out of the backseat. It was rare for their mother to drive them anywhere.

"Thanks, Daddy," Davia cooed as she emerged from the front seat. "And thank you for agreeing to the party."

"Party?" Drew asked.

"The sleepover, Daddy," Davia corrected herself.

"Fine."

The twins closed the car doors and made their way across the parking lot.

"I can't believe you still call him 'daddy.'"

Davia flicked her long blond hair over her shoulder. "You can't believe I get my way more than you do. So, is she your girlfriend now?" Davia asked. "Did you two make out at the movie? Did your hands wander to —"

"Can it, Davia."

"Someone's testy. Maybe she hasn't kissed you at all," Davia teased. "Maybe you'll never get a girlfriend. And that's the difference between us. If I wanted to be in a relationship, I would be."

"I said can it." Darius split off from Davia and walked toward the bus drop off. He grimaced, frustrated he had let her goad him. He and Adelaide had kissed, just not last night. A smile crept across his face as he recalled the handful of times she had kissed him. Each time they had been solving mysteries. He needed another case.

***

The mall parking lot was almost deserted. Only a handful of cars, all belonging to mall employees, were peppered throughout the parking lot. Belinda pulled a tube of red lipstick from her purse. She looked in the rearview mirror and touched up her lips. Satisfied, she dropped the lipstick back into her purse and climbed out of the beat-up K-car. She smoothed her skirt, adjusted the shoulder pads in her cream blouse, and strode across the lot to the mall entrance.

Belinda walked through the doors and down the almost vacant corridors. Her pumps tapped across the brown tile floor. Metal security doors clacked open as employees opened the shops.

She stopped short at the Kinkos. There was a single piece of paper taped to the storefront. Belinda blinked.

The handwritten sign read, "This location is permanently closed."

Belinda leaned against the metal door to steady herself. It shuddered, the metal panels adjusting to her weight.

"No," Belinda whispered. "No, no, no."

Two

The low hum of chatter filled the classroom as Mr. McKenzie's students ate their lunches. Adelaide closed her eyes and savoured the flavours in her leftover slice of pizza. Even cold, the capocollo, spicy pepper and olive-topped pizza slice was delicious.

"That looks good," Tetsu said. He craned his neck to get a better look.

Adelaide opened her eyes. "Trade?" she asked as she picked up the second slice and held it out to him. She nodded toward his sushi.

"No take backs!" Tetsu snatched the pizza out of her hand.

"That's fine." Adelaide took half a dozen salmon uramaki out of Tetsu's container.

"Your lunches have been better lately," Tetsu observed. "I like your mom's new job."

"It pays better I guess." Adelaide shrugged. Her mother's new job included a steady paycheque, which had reduced the number of peanut butter and jam sandwiches.

Adelaide gestured at the sushi. "These are good."

"You don't have to eat rice for every meal," Tetsu grumbled. He turned to the pizza slice and grinned.

"Neither do you," Adelaide pointed out.

"Only 'cause I've got you, friend." Tetsu took a big bite of pizza and closed his eyes in pleasure. "Oh, that's the stuff," he garbled as he chewed.

"You only eat rice?" Darius asked.

"Only rice." Tetsu nodded.

Darius looked at Adelaide who gave a slight shake of her head.

"Wait, what's on this?" Tetsu asked.

"Capocollo," Adelaide replied.

"It's spicy."

"I like spicy food," Adelaide reminded him.

"You're so weird. But it *is* pizza." Tetsu looked at the slice of pizza and smiled again.

"Tetsu's family eats a traditional Japanese diet, which includes a lot of rice. Don't let him fool you, though, it isn't all sushi. Which is good, by the way." Adelaide gave Tetsu a pointed look. "Plus, he eats cereal at my house every weekend."

"Did, uh, did Davia invite you over for the sleepover?" Darius asked Adelaide.

"What sleepover?" Adelaide looked around as though the classroom held the answers.

"I'd say that's a no," Tetsu offered. He gnawed on the pizza crust with a blissful look on his face.

"Helpful," Kurt noted as he looked up from the copy of *The Fellowship of the Ring* he'd checked out of the city library.

Adelaide realized Sophie was strangely quiet and stole a look in her direction. Sophie took another bite of her sandwich and remained silent.

"What about you?" Tetsu asked Sophie. "Everyone knows Adelaide hates girl stuff. You get an invite?"

"No." Sophie's gaze flicked to Tetsu and her eyes narrowed.

"All righty then," Tetsu said. He turned back to Adelaide. "What else you got in that lunch kit?"

***

Miranda Belcouer lurked next to her two-seater Porsche 911 Turbo.

"See you tomorrow?" Darius looked at Adelaide hopefully.

Adelaide nodded. "Yes, I'll be here."

"Right, of course." It had been a stupid thing to say. Of course, Darius would see her at school tomorrow. He glanced toward the parking lot where his mother offered a tentative wave. He waved back. "Have a good night," he said to Adelaide, trying to sound more confident.

"You too," Adelaide replied. She gave him a small smile and headed for the yellow school bus that would take her home.

Darius checked for moving vehicles, then walked across the parking lot.

"Hi, Darius," Miranda said as he approached. She smiled tightly, as though her face didn't know how to be happy. Darius recalled once, back in Boston, when she'd come in from a night out with some other woman giggling and laughing. She'd looked buoyant, though quite drunk. His father had been unimpressed.

"Hi, Mom," Darius replied. He smiled broadly at her, and meant it. It wasn't often they were alone. He was looking forward to the drive.

Miranda's smile deepened and looked slightly more sincere.

Darius opened the car door and slipped into the passenger seat.

"How was your day?" Miranda asked as she opened

her door and took a seat behind the wheel.

"It was good! How was yours?" Darius asked as he fastened his seatbelt.

"Oh, the same as always I suppose," she murmured. Her smile faltered slightly. "I'm glad your day was good. It's nice to see you!" She started the car.

"Thanks, Mom," Darius said.

Miranda carefully eased the car out of the parking stall, checking the mirrors constantly. Darius always marvelled at how different of a driver she was compared to his father.

"I haven't heard anything from your teachers," Miranda said, carefully.

Darius tried not to sigh. "Everything is going good, Mom. I'm not getting in fights. I promise."

"Okay, Darius. I just want you to be happy, you know?" Miranda glanced over and gave Darius a tight smile.

"Thanks, Mom." Darius couldn't help but wonder if she even knew how to be happy, if either of his parents did. Darius had seen Adelaide and her mother together a few times now, and while their relationship probably had its problems, he was intrigued by how casual their conversations were.

"Of course," Miranda said. She reached over and patted Darius leg before she turned her full attention back to the road. The rest of the drive was quiet, an uneasy air of questions unasked and unanswered.

***

Tetsu, Kurt and Adelaide got off the bus at the corner of Hickory Avenue and Pine Street. Adelaide frowned as she looked up the street at her house. Her mother's K-car was parked in the driveway. The three of them walked in silence until they reached Kurt's house. It was a sad one-storey home with empty flower beds.

"See you tomorrow, Kurt." Adelaide gave a small wave.

"See you guys!" Kurt waved back as he turned up the front walk.

Adelaide and Tetsu continued up the street.

"Isn't she supposed to be at work?" Tetsu asked.

"Mmmhmm," Adelaide murmured.

"Well, that ain't good."

"Maybe she came home sick."

"Yeah, okay." Tetsu clapped Adelaide on her back. "I'll take off. Call me if you need me." Tetsu walked to the side gate and let himself into her backyard. From there, Adelaide knew, he would use the back gate to cut through the woods and emerge on his own street a few houses over.

Adelaide sighed and walked up her front steps. She used her key to open the front door and stepped inside.

"Mama? Hello?" Adelaide slipped off her shoes. "I'm home."

"I'm in here, baby." Belinda's voice was hollow.

Adelaide entered the living room, which was adjacent to the front foyer. Her mother lay sprawled on the couch in sweatpants and an oversized T-shirt. She was holding a half-eaten pint of Ben & Jerry's Cherry Garcia ice cream.

Adelaide's stomach dropped. "What happened?"

"I don't know." Belinda looked down at the carton and then back up at Adelaide. "I went to work, baby. I promise. I was doing good. So good."

"Did they ..." Adelaide paused, choosing her words carefully. "Did they let you go for some reason?"

"No. I don't think so." Belinda licked the back of the spoon. "They were just gone. They closed up overnight."

"Did you forget they told you they were closing?"

Adelaide racked her brain for anything her mother might have mentioned and then forgotten.

"Vernon said I was doing great. Last night he said 'see you tomorrow' when I left." Belinda scooped a melty glob of fudge onto her spoon. "They're just gone." She lifted the spoon to her mouth. "I'm unemployed. Again."

Adelaide took a deep breath and closed her eyes.

Three

The early morning sun made a half-hearted attempt to shine through the grey clouds overhead. Adelaide guessed it would be raining by recess.

"Morning!" Kurt offered as he fell in step with Tetsu and Adelaide.

"Hi, Kurt," Adelaide replied absently. She was lost in thought about her mother.

Sophie stomped out of the house and slammed the front door behind her. Kurt winced. Tetsu raised his eyebrows, then looked at the ground and started to walk toward the bus stop. Everyone kept pace with him. They walked in silence for two houses.

"I cannot believe them!" Sophie huffed.

"We're doing this then," Tetsu mumbled under his breath. "Cool."

Sophie had a tendency for dramatics and there was usually no way to console her.

Kurt frowned at Tetsu. He turned to Sophie and put his hand on her arm. "Do you want to talk about it?"

"No!" Sophie snapped. "The girls at practice are stupid. They are so stupid and they don't even know how to play volleyball as well as me."

Kurt opened his mouth and closed it again. "What happened?" he asked instead.

"I told you,"—Sophie wheeled on him—"I don't want to talk about it! They chatted away and giggled all practice. They were making fun of me. I know it! And all of them are invited to this stupid sleepover. All of them except *me*!"

Adelaide remained quiet. She found the best tactic was just to let Sophie get it all out.

"This is not talking about it?" Tetsu muttered.

"Shut up, Tetsu!" Sophie snapped.

"Adelaide isn't invited," Kurt pointed out.

"She isn't on the team, Kurt!" Sophie howled. Then she grimaced. "I'm sorry, Kurt. It isn't your fault. It's just"—Sophie looked over at Adelaide—"no offence, but you aren't on the team or anything."

"None taken." Adelaide shrugged. "I'm really sorry, Sophie. That sucks."

"You have no idea!" Sophie exclaimed.

The four of them waited at the bus stop and, before too long, the yellow bus trundled down the road, pulled over and opened its doors. They filed in, Adelaide and Tetsu sat down in the frontmost bench on the same side as the door. Kurt plunked down onto the seat just behind them.

"Kurt!" Julie called from several rows back. "Kurt, you can sit here!"

Kurt ignored Julie's offer and sat down in his usual seat behind Adelaide and Tetsu.

Sophie, who had boarded the bus last, moved to sit with Julie.

"Take a seat please," the bus driver called.

Adelaide glanced toward the back of the bus where Julie seemed to be trying to convince Sophie she needed the extra space for her backpack. This was definitely new.

"So?" Tetsu asked.

Adelaide took a deep breath and turned back to Tetsu. Sophie's drama had been a welcome distraction.

"You didn't say what happened with your mom," Tetsu pressed.

Adelaide glanced back and saw that Julie had grudgingly allowed Sophie to sit with her.

"What happened with your mom, Adelaide?" Kurt leaned forward to peer over the top of the seat.

"She lost her job." Adelaide's voice was flat, but her

stomach twisted into a knot. Belinda had spent whatever money she had earned. It was mid-October. Without a job, no money would come in until the rent cheques on the first of November.

"Ha! I knew it!" Tetsu clapped his hand over his mouth. "I'm sorry, it just came out."

"It's fine," Adelaide said. "She had a good run there. Over two weeks."

"Why'd they let her go this time?" Kurt asked.

"The place closed. I told her to call head office and ask about it. I'm pretty sure they should have at least mentioned it."

"Are you sure they didn't? I just mean …" Kurt trailed off.

"I know what you mean," Adelaide said. "It's okay." She looked past Kurt at Sophie and Julie. Sophie had a scowl across her face. She imagined Sophie's drama would become the centerpiece of conversation at lunch.

"If there's anything we can do …" Kurt looked at Tetsu and then back at Adelaide.

"Thanks, Kurt. I appreciate it. We'll figure it out. We always do."

The rest of the ride passed in silence.

***

Darius grinned as Adelaide stepped off the school bus. Her wrist cuff peeked out from under the sleeve of her pink raincoat. There was something about it that just suited her.

Tetsu, who had exited the bus just before Adelaide, glanced in Darius' direction and then said something. Adelaide looked up. She didn't smile exactly, but Darius liked to think her face softened just a bit, that her eyes lit up. He hoped it wasn't his imagination.

Kurt stepped off the bus next, and Darius caught up with them as they moved toward the school building. He glanced back to see if Sophie would join them, but the trio continued to walk and Sophie exited the bus with Julie. He had enough experience with girls to know Sophie was in a bad mood and he quickened his pace to keep up with the others.

"So, listen, I was thinking," Darius started.

"Good morning, Darius," Adelaide said.

"Oh, um, yeah. Hi! Good morning," Darius replied, embarrassed he hadn't greeted her properly before.

"Hi yourself," Tetsu retorted. It was half-hearted, and Darius hoped he was slowly winning over

Adelaide's best friend.

"Morning, Tetsu, Kurt. So, I was thinking," Darius started again, "this whole thing with Grover Jergen. We didn't get to the bottom of it. There must be something else we can do."

"He's probably dead, from what you two were saying, anyway," Tetsu said. "I bet those feds wacked him."

"Wacked him?" Darius asked.

"Don't you watch movies? Yeah, the guy was bad news and feds *took care of him*, you know?" He dragged his hand across his throat as he enunciated for effect.

"The feds?" Kurt asked.

"Those agents," Tetsu waved his hand. "The National Parks people. If that's who they really were."

Darius frowned. It hadn't sat right with him that the two men in suits, who had been by the so-called haunted house with a Frankenstein's monster in the basement, actually worked for The National Park Services. Even if that's when their ID had said. Even if there was a poster of Smokey Bear in their office. "So, you agree something's off?"

"That's not what I said," Tetsu retorted.

Adelaide sighed. "Do you think it's weird or not?"

"Fine," Tetsu grumbled. "The whole thing is weird."

"Okay," Darius continued, somewhat satisfied. "We didn't get to the bottom of Grover Jergen. Did they find him? Is he still out there? What about the birds?"

"You should leave it," Tetsu said. "Don't mess with stuff you don't understand. Especially cops, feds and anyone impersonating 'em."

Darius tried not to roll his eyes. "I want answers. Notices of death should be in the paper, right?"

"Obituaries? Sometimes, sure," Kurt said. "But if you missed it, do your parents keep copies of old papers? Or get ones from out of town?"

"No." Darius grimaced.

"The library would have them. Not this one," Kurt said as he gestured to the school. "The public one."

"Yeah?" Darius asked. He was excited at the possibility of some answers.

"I'm sure. My mom works there part-time," Kurt explained. "Plus, I like it there. There are so many books!"

Darius chuckled. "Thanks, Kurt. Maybe I'll check it out today. Anyone in?" He looked hopefully at Adelaide.

"I'm sorry, Darius. I have to get home after school," she said, distracted.

Darius tried not to let his disappointment show.

"Well, um, I'll tell you what I find?"

"Yes. Sure. Thank you."

"I can come," Kurt said. "Probably. You'll need help navigating your way around there anyway. All the librarians know me."

Darius smiled. "Thanks, Kurt. That'd be great."

***

After school, the quartet of friends filed off the bus, with Tetsu in the lead. Kurt followed Adelaide, and Sophie was a bit behind them, her seat farther back having delayed her departure. The day had dragged on and Adelaide had mixed feelings about returning home.

"I'm surprised you didn't say yes to the library with Darius," Kurt commented as they walked up the road.

"Me too," Adelaide replied.

"It's about your mom?" Kurt asked lightly.

Adelaide nodded. "I should get home and keep an eye on her. You know how she gets when she's like this."

Kurt set his lips in a grim line and nodded. Tetsu put an arm around Adelaide.

"See you guys," Sophie said as she broke off and strode up the walkway.

"That's real support there," Tetsu muttered quietly.

"It's fine. I think Amy is supposed to call her today," Adelaide said.

"Not Amy Pecora?" Tetsu gasped mockingly.

"Hush, you," Adelaide said. "You know Sophie's missed her ever since her parents split up and she had to leave Olympic Vista. It'll be nice for them to talk."

Sophie may have spent time with Julie and the other popular girls, but it was art-loving Amy who had been Sophie's best friend. The move had devasted Sophie and Adelaide thought that contributed to Sophie's mood swings.

"I guess," Tetsu said, doubtfully. He dropped his arm around Adelaide as they paused at Kurt's house. The Zillman car wasn't in the driveway, but a figure stood in the front window watching them.

Adelaide glanced at the disapproving face of Agatha Zillman and turned back to her friends. "I don't want Sophie feeling sorry for me, anyway," Adelaide added.

"No one feels sorry for you, Adelaide," Kurt assured her. "We just care."

Adelaide smiled at him. "Thanks, Kurt. Good luck at the library. I hope you guys find something."

"I'll let you know," Kurt promised. He waved

goodbye as he walked up the front walk to his door.

Adelaide returned the wave and did her best to ignore Agatha. She turned and walked alongside Tetsu toward her house. Adelaide didn't think she had ever done anything to hurt or offend Kurt or his mother. Her own mother once told her that it was impossible to make everyone happy and there were some people you shouldn't bother trying to appease. Adelaide often wished her mother would at least try a little with Agatha. It would have made her friendship with Kurt easier.

"How can I help?" Tetsu asked.

"Hmm?" Adelaide asked as Tetsu broke her from her thoughts.

"Your mom. What can I do?"

"Oh, nothing. Thank you, though. I'm going to try to get to the bottom of it. Maybe I can get in touch with someone. It's a company. There are other offices. Someone has to have answers."

"Good thinkin'. Want me to make some calls with you?" Tetsu asked.

Adelaide smiled inwardly at the idea of Tetsu convincing any corporation to give him information over the phone. "Thank you. I appreciate it. I can do it, though. And I know you are trying to avoid your

Japanese lessons."

"Come on!" Tetsu scrunched his face in disappointment. "I can speak Japanese. And you need me."

Adelaide was amused by his expression, which reminded her of a small child pouting. It was a look she was too familiar with, though he never made it in front of anyone else.

"I do need you, but not to make phone calls. Your mom doesn't think your pronunciation is good enough. Go." Adelaide pointed toward the gate on the side of her house. "I'm not having your mother mad at me."

"Fine," Tetsu huffed. "But I offered!"

Adelaide waved him off and walked up the rotting front steps to her large old house. She took a breath and opened the door.

"Baby? Is that you?" Belinda called from the couch in the living room.

"Yes, Mama." Adelaide slipped off her shoes and stowed them in the hall closet. She padded through the large doorway into the living room and pursed her lips. Her mother lay on the couch in an oversized T-shirt. There was an open bag of O'Grady's au gratin chips on the table.

"It's nice to see you, baby."

Belinda, and the floor, were covered in chip crumbs. Yesterday's makeup was smeared across Belinda's face.

"It's nice to see you, Mama. Did you call head office like I suggested?"

"What's the point?" Belinda wallowed.

Adelaide sighed. "Are you hungry?"

"Not really. Maybe?" Belinda glanced at the empty bag. "Yes. I can make something."

"It's not dinner yet. I'll make us a snack."

"You don't have to, baby. I'm the parent." Belinda started to push herself off the couch.

"I want to," Adelaide insisted. It had to be her idea. "Really."

"If you're sure. I don't know what I did to deserve you."

Adelaide patted her hand. "I'll be back in a minute."

She collected the garbage off the table and retreated to the kitchen. Before too long, Adelaide set a plate of crackers smeared with peanut butter on the coffee table. She sat down next to her mother.

"How was school?" Belinda asked as she picked up a cracker.

"It was fine," Adelaide said. "Mr. McKenzie is

reading *Watership Down* to us."

"That's nice," Belinda replied. She popped the cracker in her mouth.

"Yes," Adelaide agreed. "He has a good voice for reading aloud." She picked up her own cracker and took a small bite. She wondered what sort of after school snack Mrs. Katillion had made for Sophie and Andy.

"How's Darius?" Belinda asked.

"He's okay," Adelaide said, grateful her mother was forgetting her woes, even briefly. Adelaide didn't want to admit she had abandoned him to keep an eye on her. "I think he likes it here."

"In small town Olympic Vista?"

"Yes, Mama, in small town Olympic Vista."

Belinda's eyes twinkled. "I'm not surprised," she said, appraising her daughter.

"What does that mean?" Adelaide asked with a small frown.

"It means that the hustle and bustle of an amazing city like Boston pales in comparison to you, baby."

"Okay," Adelaide said skeptically. She thought of reminding her mother she'd never been to Boston, but she thought better of it. Her mother was too fragile for teasing right now. "Have another cracker."

"Don't mind if I do," Belinda said as she picked up another one.

"Davia is hosting a sleepover tonight," Adelaide said.

"Oh? And? When do I have to take you there?"

"I'm not going." Adelaide picked up another cracker. "It's for the volleyball team, which I'm not on." She frowned slightly as she thought of Sophie being excluded, then she took a bite of the cracker.

"Do you wish you'd joined the team?" Belinda asked as she picked up another cracker.

"Oh, no. That's not it," Adelaide said, realizing her mother thought she was upset about her own lack of an invitation. "Sophie wasn't invited. I think Davia was making a point, I'm just not sure what. Or why."

"Because she can. Girls are the worst. Except you. You are wonderful." Belinda took a bite of her cracker.

"You have to say that. You're my mother."

Belinda wrinkled her nose. "Do I? You are so much better than I was at your age," Belinda said. "So much better than I am even now."

"Why don't you have the last cracker?" Adelaide suggested. They were wandering into dangerous territory now and Adelaide had other plans.

"Oh, sure, baby." Belinda picked up the last cracker.

"Maybe I'll host a sleepover where Sophie is invited," Adelaide suggested.

Belinda's eyes sparkled and she sat up straighter. "That would be fun!" She clapped her hands together. "I could make pancakes for you girls! And you could stay up late gossiping and painting your nails."

Adelaide nodded. She hated gossip, and wasn't overly fond of painted nails, but this would mean a lot to her mother and to Sophie. "Soon then. But not yet. I can't try to compete with Davia's party."

"Good thinking. You're good at this," Belinda marvelled.

Adelaide collected the plate and stood up. "We should call head office now. There's still time."

"Adelaide, no. No, there's no point," Belinda objected. She flopped back on the couch.

"Fine. I'll do it myself." And, hearing no objections, Adelaide did just that.

Four

Darius looked back and forth across the parking lot of the public library. Kurt pedalled into view, slightly out of breath.

Darius waved enthusiastically. "Thanks for doing this, Kurt!" Darius greeted him.

"Sure thing. I can't be too long. I mean the library closes soon anyway, but I have to be home before my dad gets home." Kurt climbed off his bike and wheeled it to the building where he leaned it against the wall. "Where's your bike?"

"My dad dropped me off." Darius recalled how unimpressed his father had been at making another stop. "Should get started if you have to get home to your dad." It was nice to know he wasn't alone in having an unpleasant father.

"Yeah, sure."

They walked to the glass-doored entry, pulled open the heavy doors, and stepped into the library. It was smaller than any library Darius was used to, except maybe the school library. He looked around, uncertain where to start. The room had tall ceilings and, on the left, there was a mezzanine with several doors. He looked around for stairs, but couldn't see any.

"Come on," Kurt said, leading the way past the checkout desk and through the stacks. He waved at a few people as he walked and they waved back. Inside the library, surrounded by so many books, Kurt looked more relaxed than Darius was used to. They walked to the area under the mezzanine where assorted magazines and newspapers were displayed on shelves.

"What's upstairs?" Darius asked.

"Mostly storage, but there is a meeting room sort of thing up there, too. It's off limits for visitors, but my mom let me up there once. It isn't that exciting." He scanned the shelves and moved toward the Seattle Post-Intelligencer. He paused. "The stairs are close to the checkout area. Behind a door."

"Thanks," Darius said, somewhat satisfied. "But we don't need to go up there?"

"No, everything should be right here." Kurt pulled a few papers off the racks they were stored on, and walked over to a table.

They opened the papers, one at a time, and scanned

the obituaries. It took a while, but then Darius saw it. It was a small article, not an obituary at all.

The headline read, "Home Invasion Ends in Fatality," but nothing about the article read like a home invasion. A small trailer had been ransacked. There had been no leads. The deceased had been confirmed as Grover Jergen, PhD.

"There it is," Darius said. "I guess they got him."

"You don't think it was a home invasion?" Kurt asked.

"Adelaide and I saw, well, an order on this guy. They were supposed to 'eliminate him if he's trouble.' And I guess they did."

The two sat in silence, staring at the paper.

***

Adelaide frowned. She pulled the receiver away from her ear, looked at it, then held it back to her ear again. "I'm sorry, can you repeat that?"

"We don't have a record of Kinkos in Olympic Vista," the male voice said through the phone.

"I saw it in the mall," Adelaide insisted. "I used it." That was a lie, of course, but she wasn't about to admit she was calling on behalf of her mother.

"I'm very sorry, ma'am," the male said. "We have no record of any Kinkos franchise in that area. There are two in Seattle, and one in Olympia if you'd like to visit either of them."

Adelaide's frown deepened. She'd seen the storefront. She'd watched people go in and out of the copy store. And yet, the head of human resources didn't sound like he was lying. "You're sure?"

"Ma'am, I'm uncertain where you were getting your printing done in this, Olympic Vista? But we don't have a Kinkos there." He sounded almost as confused as she felt.

There was a long pause.

"Well, thank you for your help," Adelaide finally said. "I hope you have a nice evening."

"You as well, ma'am."

Adelaide set the receiver back into its cradle and blinked.

A shadow moved in the kitchen doorway.

"Any luck, baby?" Belinda asked.

Adelaide shook her head.

Five

Adelaide and Tetsu sat on the worn hardwood floor in her living room. She lifted a spoonful of Honey Nut Cheerios to her mouth. Tetsu slurped cereal off his spoon.

The week was finally over and the two of them were partaking in one of their favourite weekend pastimes: Saturday morning cartoons and sugary cereal. Adelaide was at a loss about what to do about her mother's job, so the two of them sat, transfixed by the television where the little blue Smurfs had been transported to an evil dream world by the wicked sorcerer, Morphio.

Footfalls behind them caused Adelaide to divert her gaze. Rico, her mother's current boyfriend, entered the room.

"Get me some cereal," he ordered as he strode to the green tweed sofa.

Tetsu glanced over and pointed at himself with a confused look on his face.

Rico nodded as he blinked rapidly.

It was a trait that left Adelaide unsettled. Her

stomach turned as he sat down.

The show cut to commercials and Tetsu clambered to his feet.

"You cried last night," Rico stated as though it was a matter of fact. He glanced at Adelaide and then looked over at the television.

Adelaide frowned and recalled her night. The phone call hadn't gone as she had hoped, but she was sure Rico hadn't been here and she certainly hadn't cried about it.

"That wasn't me," Adelaide said. She made an effort to remove any emotion from her voice. She hated when the men in her mother's life told her they didn't like her tone. Then again, she hated when anyone told her that.

"Yes, it was. I heard you. You can talk about your emotions and problems with me." Rico turned and smiled at her. Adelaide suspected it was meant to be reassuring, but his lips stretched in a forced and unnatural way and there was something strange about his word selection.

"Okay, but it wasn't me," Adelaide repeated. "It was Violet. She cries a lot." Violet was one of their roommates. Adelaide looked over at the door into the foyer. She hoped Tetsu didn't take much longer in the kitchen. She turned back to the television screen as the Keebler elves threw buckets of chocolate at assorted cookies.

"It's okay to feel something," Rico assured her.

Adelaide tried not to grit her teeth. The front door opened and she turned in the direction of the front foyer.

"Howdy," Waylon, their other roommate, said as he entered the room. His cowboy boots clomped on the wooden floor. "I thought I heard them cartoons."

Adelaide looked up in his direction. Waylon always smelled of leather and musk. Adelaide found it comforting, even when it was mixed with stale cigarettes and beer, as it often was when he finished a night shift at a club in nearby Olympia.

"Why are you coming in so early?" Rico asked Waylon.

"Well, I'm just home from work," Waylon explained. He glanced over at Adelaide with a slight eyeroll.

"You stink of beer. Seems to me a respectable person wouldn't stink of liquor at this hour of the morning." Rico blinked rapidly.

Waylon nodded for a moment. "Well, partner, seems to me used car salesmen aren't all that respectable neither." He stepped toward Adelaide. "I brought this home for ya. Vending machine gave me two of 'em." He handed Adelaide a Baby Ruth chocolate bar.

Tetsu reappeared in the door with two bowls of cereal. He shoved one bowl at Rico, nodded at Waylon, and then returned to his seat on the floor.

Rico raised his eyebrows at Waylon. He continued to blink rapidly as he lifted a spoonful of cereal to his mouth. "Ugh! What is this?" he exclaimed.

Waylon chuckled and walked out of the room. "Have a good one, Adelaide!" he called over his shoulder. "See ya 'round, Tetsu!"

"Cereal," Tetsu said to Rico before he shrugged and turned back to the television.

Waylon's heavy foot falls could be heard ascending the staircase.

"How can you eat this?" Rico asked with a sour expression.

"Just do." Tetsu didn't avert his gaze from the screen.

"Rico, you wanted me to talk about my feelings? I'm feeling frustrated you are making so much noise." Adelaide gestured to the television where Papa Smurf negotiated with the Sandman to enter the dream world.

"You shouldn't speak to me like that," Rico warned. He clinked his spoon against the bowl loudly as he set it down on the coffee table. He leaned back on the couch and put his feet up next to the bowl.

"Okay." Adelaide sighed. "Enjoy the cartoons and cereal, Rico." She stood up. "Come on, Tetsu."

Tetsu sighed and climbed to his feet. He picked up his bowl of cereal off the floor and followed her out of the room.

"Sorry, Tetsu. Cartoons won't be fun now," Adelaide said as she carried her empty bowl to the kitchen. "And I was a bit distracted anyway."

"I know," Tetsu agreed. "But you can't stop me from finishing this cereal. And I know you got a chocolate bar. I can smell it. You'll have to share that."

"That's fine," Adelaide said. She gave Tetsu a small smile as they walked back to the kitchen. "Bike ride? We could see what comics they have."

"Yeah," Tetsu replied. "Maybe they'll have the newest issue of *Conan the Barbarian*."

***

Darius sat on the floor of the pool house with his legs tucked under the coffee table.

There was a brief knock at the door, and then it opened to reveal his mother. She wore jeans and a light blue blouse. She had pulled on a trench coat and the shoulders of it were speckled with tiny wet spots.

"Darius, dear," Miranda said. "There's a phone call for you."

"Really?" Darius looked up from *The Swamp Monster*, one of the more recent Hardy Boys books he'd acquired.

"Yes, it's Adelaide," Miranda replied.

"Yeah?" Darius' heart skipped a beat. He scrambled to his feet so quickly, he banged his knee on the coffee table. He sucked in his breath. She hadn't wanted to go to the library with him, and then she hadn't been at Davia's sleepover. But she was calling, so that had to be a good sign.

"I'm sure she can wait a moment," Miranda said. There was a tinge of amusement to her voice. "Are you all right?"

"Fine, I'm fine," Darius assured her. His leg smarted. He ran his fingers through his hair as he walked briskly from the pool house back to the main house. The rain had eased up, which was good because in his haste, Darius had left his jacket in the pool house.

The phone receiver lay on the counter, tethered to the wall by a long cord.

"Hello?" Darius asked, slightly out of breath.

"Hello. This is Adelaide. Is this Darius?"

"Adelaide, yeah, this is Darius. Hi, um, how's it going?" Darius asked. He ran his hand through his hair again. He heard his mother step in through the side door, then the door closed. His eyes stayed focused on the wall, but he was picturing Adelaide with her long dark hair and solemn face. She was probably sitting at the banquette in her kitchen. He remembered eating Kraft Mac and Cheese Dinner there.

"Darius?"

"What, yeah, I'm here!" Darius said. He wondered if he'd been so busy thinking about her, he'd gotten distracted.

"I asked if you're free tomorrow. A store at the mall closed and it shouldn't have. It doesn't make sense."

"I'm free. When do you need me?" Darius couldn't believe his luck. He wouldn't have to wait until Monday to see her again.

"The mall doesn't open until noon on Sundays, so noon." Her voice was serious, but calm and even.

Darius could listen to her for hours. "Noon. Got it."

"Okay." She paused. "Enjoy the rest of your day."

"Um, yeah? Thanks! You too?" Darius wasn't sure

exactly what to say. He didn't want her to hang up yet.

"Okay. Bye." There was a click and the line went dead.

Darius stared at the receiver and then hung it up.

"Is everything all right?" Miranda asked.

Darius turned. "Yeah, um, I think so." Adelaide had called him. She wanted his help. He grinned. "It's great. It's okay if I go meet my friends at the mall tomorrow, right?"

"The mall here is open on a Sunday? Isn't that charming."

"It sounds like it," Darius said.

"I imagine your sister will be happy about that. Well, I don't see why that would be a problem," Miranda replied with a smile.

"Thanks, Mom!" Darius paused. "She's strangely formal on the phone," he said, absently.

"I noticed that. I was impressed. Good phone etiquette is important."

"I suppose so," Darius said, slightly puzzled. He realized he wasn't even sure what tomorrow's mission was about.

"Oh, there's a costume shop called Dizzy Izzy's Costume Emporium that's opened in town. I saw a charming little ad for it in the newspaper. I was going to pick up something there for you for Halloween. Any requests?"

"Um …" Darius was distracted as he replayed the conversation with Adelaide in his head.

"Darius?" Miranda asked. "The good costumes will be gone if you don't decide, dear."

"A … football player?" Darius suggested. He thought it would be ironic given he had never overly enjoyed team sports.

"All right. I'll see what I can find. Apparently, it has the 'best fright-ses.' I'm not even sure if that's a word."

"Thanks, Mom," Darius said absently. What had Adelaide said? There was something about a store, and it being closed. That was all he knew. Tomorrow could not come soon enough.

Six

Dry leaves flicked across the mall parking lot as the wind picked up. Darius locked up his bike at one of the bike racks. He wasn't used to bike racks at malls, or anywhere other than school really, but when it came to Olympic Vista, bike racks at the mall seemed to be the smallest of the oddities.

There were only a few unfamiliar bikes tucked into the rack. Darius wondered if the others had used the bike rack on the other side of the mall. He hoped they hadn't abandoned the mission or followed the trail elsewhere without him.

Darius walked briskly to the mall entrance, opened the heavy glass doors, and stepped inside. He walked along the long black mats by the entrance, then stepped on the brown tile floor. Darius' runners squeaked on the tiles so he moved back onto the mat and rubbed his shoes along them to remove as much of the moisture as he could. He ran his tongue across his teeth.

Darius had grinned the whole way there. At one

point a bug had flown straight at him and he had almost swallowed it.

He found Adelaide, Sophie, and Tetsu at the food court. They sat around an empty table deep in conversation. He wondered where Kurt was.

Adelaide looked up as he approached. "I'm glad you could make it." She smiled at him.

"Wouldn't miss it!" Darius ran his hand through his hair. "Does anyone want anything?" He gestured toward the Dunkin' Donuts and the Orange Julius.

Tetsu's eyes brightened.

"After we're done. We've got work to do first," Adelaide said firmly as she looked at Tetsu. She turned back to Darius. "But thank you."

"Of course. Sure." Darius nodded and took a seat.

"Hi, Darius." Sophie beamed at him.

"Hi, Sophie," Darius replied. He gave her a quick nod and turned back to Adelaide. "So, I was confused on the phone. What's going on?"

"It's complicated, I think," Adelaide started.

"Her mom lost her job because the place is gone," Tetsu offered.

"It's more than that." Adelaide frowned at Tetsu. "My mom has been working at the Kinkos for a couple of weeks," she explained to Darius. "She was really proud of it. Then on Wednesday she went to work and the doors were closed and locked. The place was empty. There wasn't a copy machine in sight."

Darius nodded, trying to understand. "They didn't give her any notice? You know, tell her the shop was closing?"

"No. One day they said they'd see her the next day. The next day, she came home confused because it was suddenly closed. I told her she should call head office and find out what's going on."

"And?" Darius asked.

"And so, Adelaide called head office," Tetsu chimed in.

"Shh." Adelaide swatted Tetsu's arm. "Head office has no record of there even being a Kinkos here in Olympic Vista. Something weird is going on."

"He, or she, human resources, I mean … do you think they were lying?" Darius asked.

"I don't think so," Adelaide replied.

"Okay. How was she paid?" Darius asked, confused.

"Yeah, so they paid her with personal cheques!" Tetsu laughed. "Oh, Belinda. Nothing says professional print shop like a handwritten cheque from some guy named Vernon."

"Stop that!" Adelaide frowned and swatted him again. "I didn't know," she added quietly.

"Cut it out, Tetsu," Darius said. "We should divide and conquer."

Tetsu balked.

"Whoa, I've got this," Tetsu said. He puffed out his chest and looked around the table at Sophie, Adelaide and, lastly, Darius. "We should divide and conquer. Sophie, you check around the nearby stores. Isn't there a woman's clothing store there? And Adelaide you can talk to the people who rent the stores out."

"You mean the administration who rent the storefronts? They're probably closed today," Adelaide cut in. "I wish I'd thought of this Friday. We might not get far. This might be a job for tomorrow."

"Today. You'll figure something out." Tetsu waved his hand. "I'm going to talk to the security guard. I bet he knows everything."

"And me?" Darius raised his eyebrow.

"Oh, you can, uh …" Tetsu looked around.

"You can help me." Adelaide smiled.

Darius grinned.

Tetsu grimaced. "Fine."

"So, I just have to go look around the Bootlegger?"

Sophie asked.

"For clues, Sophie," Tetsu reminded her.

"Yeah, fine. If anyone can manage on their own in the mall, it's me, anyway."

"I'm going to be"—Tetsu paused—"you know what, never mind. Everyone's got their tasks. Be back here in thirty minutes."

Darius tried not to roll his eyes at Tetsu's attempt at being in charge and decided to focus on being alone with Adelaide. He felt bad about her mother's job, but they had a new case. And they were alone. He fought the urge to take her hand as they made their way through the mall corridors toward the administration area.

"I'm sorry to hear about your mom's job," Darius offered.

"Thank you. And thanks for helping. It isn't even that she lost her job." Adelaide shook her head. "It's that I'm so confused how. It's weird, right?" She turned and looked at Darius.

"It sounds weird," Darius agreed. He fought the urge to grin at the sight of her and the excitement of another mystery. "We'll get you some answers. I promise."

Adelaide's steps faltered and she smiled at him. "Thanks, Darius."

"I'm here, for whatever you need." Darius smiled back.

"I should have suggested we do this on Friday. Or yesterday. I wasn't thinking, and then yesterday Sophie had some sports stuff."

"Sports stuff?"

"She's on some non-school teams," Adelaide explained. "She's often busy on Saturdays. And Kurt couldn't be here today because it's Sunday and his mom takes him to church." She paused. "Do you think we can get to the bottom of this?"

"Yes," Darius said confidently. He didn't feel nearly as confident as he sounded, but he was desperate to help Adelaide and her mom. A whole store seemed to have disappeared and he had to figure out how.

"Okay. Here," Adelaide said as they reached a corridor that branched off from the main thoroughfare of the mall.

They turned and walked down the empty hallway. The floor was the same brown brick-style tile as the rest of the mall, but the corridor felt different. The walls were painted stark white and were devoid of signage. The hallway had a single fire extinguisher in a cabinet and two grey doors with signs that designated them as bathrooms.

Adelaide and Darius walked past the two doors and rounded a corner.

There were two additional doors. One was labelled, "Janitorial" and the other was marked, "Administration."

"This is it," Adelaide said. She tried the office door. It was locked. She frowned and knocked. There was no answer.

Darius looked around and pulled out two paperclips. He stepped forward and winked at Adelaide.

"I've got this." He unfolded the large edge of one of the paperclips until a piece of it jutted out, then he twisted the other one into an L-shape. Darius grimaced as he wiggled the paperclips in the lock. "Almost…got…"

There was a click of heels on the tile floor.

Darius and Adelaide both paused and looked each other. He held his breath and hoped whoever it was wanted to use the bathroom.

The footsteps moved closer.

The person had almost rounded the corner. Darius looked around for somewhere to hide.

Adelaide wrapped one hand around his shoulders and pulled him into an embrace. She pushed her lips against his.

They were as soft as he remembered.

He relaxed into the kiss.

"Excuse me, what are you doing?" a woman asked.

Adelaide broke the kiss off, pulling her face away from his.

Darius blinked and ran his tongue over his upper lip. He realized his hand was empty. He didn't remember what he'd done with the paperclips.

"I'm sorry," Adelaide apologized. Her face was solemn. "I got a little caught up." Adelaide stepped to one side of the door. "Do you work here? I was hoping to ask you a couple of questions."

"I do." The woman scowled suspiciously at them. She wore a blazer and matching skirt with a blouse. Her chestnut hair, which was pulled into a severe bun, was streaked with grey. She carried a small paper cup. "We're not open today. I'm catching up on some paperwork." She fished out a ring of keys as she stepped toward the door.

Darius stepped aside to let her pass.

"You know, you really shouldn't be back here," the woman said.

"Again, I'm very sorry," Adelaide said.

The woman unlocked the door and stepped inside.

Darius waited for Adelaide to enter, but she bent

down, lifted her foot and picked up two misshapen paperclips. She smiled at him as she tucked them into her pocket.

The pair stepped out of the hallway and onto the well-worn beige carpet in the next room. The office smelled musty. The florescent light flickered and pinged. There was a large wooden desk with a computer, a multiline phone, and a pile of paperwork. Two uncomfortable looking chairs sat in front of the desk. Behind the desk was a bank of beige filing cabinets.

The woman sat in a larger chair behind the desk. She placed her paper cup down and tucked her purse into one of the desk drawers.

"It won't take long," Adelaide said. "Please."

"What are you here for?" The woman sighed. She picked up a few of the pieces of paper from the top of the pile and turned toward the cabinet.

The woman yelped and pushed her chair back without warning. It slammed into the desk. The small cup, perched too close to the edge, toppled over and landed on the floor. Brown liquid wept into the tired beige carpet.

A fat, black spider skittered across the floor and crawled between two of the cabinets.

"Shit!" the woman exclaimed. She bent down and picked up the paper cup and tossed it into the garbage can at the side of her desk. She looked up as if she had just remembered Darius and Adelaide were there. "Crap!" She clapped a hand over her mouth.

"Don't worry about us," Adelaide said. "It isn't like we haven't heard people swear before. I'm sorry about your coffee, though."

"Don't move," the woman said as she stood up and left the room with her keys.

"Maybe we should …" Darius nodded at the cabinets.

The woman's heels tapped down the corridor, then stopped.

Adelaide shook her head. "Janitor's closet," she whispered.

Darius grimaced.

Within moments the woman had returned with a brick of brown paper towels.

"Here," Darius offered, "let me help." He took the fresh stack of paper towels from her and opened the paper wrap that kept them bundled together. He pulled out a handful of paper towels and did his best to mop up the liquid.

The paper towel was drenched.

Darius tossed it into the garbage and applied more paper towel to the spot.

Adelaide crouched down next to him and together they did what they could.

"Thank you," the woman said with a sigh.

Darius gathered up the last of the coffee-soaked paper towels and dropped them into the garbage. There was still a brown stain on the carpet. His hands, and the whole room, smelled like coffee.

"You're welcome. Maybe you could you tell me who rented the Kinkos storefront? And if their lease just ended?" Adelaide asked without missing a beat. "They're closed now, but there was no sign to say they were closing."

"A store doesn't have to say they're closing, dear. They can just do it." The woman clucked as she sat back down. She glanced back to the cabinets where the spider had retreated to.

"That's fair, I suppose," Adelaide admitted. "But I was really hoping you could help us out. Maybe you can't say *who* rented it, but can you confirm if the lease is up?"

"And then you'll go?" The woman appraised them.

"And then we'll buy you a new coffee," Darius

promised as he offered his most charming smile.

The woman raised an eyebrow and nodded. She turned to fish through the cabinet drawers and pulled out a folder. She opened it and frowned. "No, that can't be right," she murmured.

"What is it?" Darius craned his neck.

She pulled the folder closer to her and tipped it up so they couldn't see it. "The lease for Kinkos ended last week."

"What else?" Adelaide pressed.

"It's just …" The woman looked up and them, and then back down at the folder. "It's just that it says I signed off on this lease. It looks like a new owner took over the store about a month ago. He took over the franchise at this location. But the lease is only for six weeks. I remember the new owner, but I didn't sign this."

"Did someone else?" Adelaide asked lightly.

"That's my signature …"

"What does that mean?" Darius pressed. "Who would have done that? And was there was a franchise here? Why'd they sell it? If you didn't sign it, who did?"

The woman scowled. "I'm not really sure I need to answer any more questions. You two should run along."

"But, please?" Darius asked. He realized he'd

pushed her too far. "The coffee?"

"I fulfilled my end of the bargain. The lease is up," the woman replied. "At least, according to the paperwork," she added in a murmur.

"But …" Darius stammered. He glanced over at Adelaide and then back at the woman.

The woman kept facing them, but she reached back, shoved the folder into a drawer with a backward glance, and closed the cabinet. "The lease was up. They didn't renew. That's all I can say."

***

Sophie and Tetsu were seated at one of the food court tables. Tetsu had a smug look about him and had leaned back in his seat as far he could. Sophie had her elbows on the table and her hands under her chin. She looked up with excitement as Darius and Adelaide slid in next to her.

"Did you have any luck?" Adelaide asked Sophie.

"I did! The girls at Bootlegger were happy to help." Sophie smiled. "Woman's clothing store." She scoffed as she turned to Tetsu. "You know they sell boys clothes, too?"

"Yeah, yeah." Tetsu waved his hand as he leaned forward. "So big news: the security guard is in on it!"

Sophie grimaced at Tetsu's interruption.

"Really?" Darius asked. "What is *it*?"

"I don't know, but he's shady and totally in on it." Tetsu nodded, obviously pleased. He reclined back in his seat and clasped his fingers behind his head.

"So, you've got nothing?" Darius asked, obviously unimpressed.

Adelaide forced herself not to smile at Darius' jab. "What have you got, Sophie?" she asked.

"Oh, me. Good! The girls at Bootlegger asked if I wanted a job. Wouldn't that be such a great place to work?" Sophie's eye lit up. "I bet I could get a discount on the great clothes!"

"*She's* got nothin'." Tetsu inclined his head at Sophie.

Adelaide knew Sophie could get a discount if she worked there. Belinda had been employed there for two months before she'd been fired because her float didn't balance. Management didn't believe someone had set her up.

"That's not true! After I explained I couldn't work there yet, I overheard them talk about Kyber from Rainy

Day Games. They said he's such a freak. And, *apparently,* he's been going down to the Kinkos after hours. He hangs out with some of the guys there. One of the girls says she saw him wearing some hooded dress thing. Total freak." She beamed at Adelaide. "That's something, right?"

"That really is. Great job, Sophie." Adelaide nodded in approval. So far it was their best lead, and Adelaide was impressed Sophie had tracked it down.

"Sorry I'm late, guys." Kurt sat down.

"How was church?" Tetsu asked.

"Fine." Kurt grimaced.

"Tetsu, please." Adelaide looked at him. Kurt didn't enjoy church, but he went because his mother made him.

"Your mom and dad make you do stuff, too," Sophie chimed it.

"And we don't tease you about it," Adelaide reminded him. She turned to Kurt. "I thought you weren't going to make it, so you aren't late. Thank you for coming."

"Fine," Tetsu sighed. "How about Darius gets us this snack he offered, and then we shake down this Kyber kid?"

Fifteen minutes later they'd updated Kurt, purchased some donuts, delivered the promised coffee to the mall administrator, and gathered by a bench near Rainy Day Games.

"We can't all go in." Darius pointed out.

"It should be Kurt," Sophie said. "He should go. This guy is supposed to be smart and really dorky." She clapped her hand over her mouth. "I'm sorry, Kurt, I just mean …"

"It's okay," Kurt replied. "I've got this. You'll come, too, Adelaide?"

"Okay." Adelaide nodded.

The two of them stepped into the store. The shelves were lined with board games: Monopoly, Clue, TROUBLE, Sorry! and Mouse Trap. In a wooden cabinet, glass chess pieces sat atop finely crafted wooden boards. One of the aisles was full of boxes of models, and another held several shelves of Lego. A table along the wall opposite the register had a working model train. Next to it was a collection of boxed train sets.

A teenager, maybe around sixteen-years-old, with red hair stood behind the counter. He looked up as they entered. He wore wrinkled clothes and had bags under his eyes. There was a jumpy look to him, as if he expected something to be lurking in the shadows.

"Hi there," Kurt said, looking up at him. "I was

hoping you could talk to me about the Dungeons and Dragons sets."

"Sure can, kid!" Kyber smiled. "Do you have any of them so far?"

"No, I don't. I'm saving up my money, though." Kurt pulled a calculator out of his pocket. "What books do I need and how much are they?"

Adelaide listened to the two of them as she moved down the first aisle to where she could see behind the counter. Under the cash register was a stack of paper bags with "Rainy Day Games" printed on them. Nothing looked out of the ordinary.

"Dude, the magic-user is the way to go, though, if you're going to play. Unless you're the Dungeon Master. That's pretty rad, too." Kyber turned and smiled at Adelaide. "Are you going to play D&D with him, too?"

"Maybe," Adelaide said. "Magic is pretty cool, huh?"

"Oh yeah!" Kyber exclaimed.

"I wish it were real," Adelaide said. This was their best lead, and she willed him to give her something to go on. She was careful to make eye contact with Kyber, the way she'd seen her mother do with men sometimes. She smiled then and looked away. "That would be really amazing." She glanced back at him.

Kyber looked around and lowered his voice. "It *is* real."

"Really?" Adelaide cocked an eyebrow.

"Oh yeah. I, uh …" Kyber glanced around the otherwise empty store. "I have a magic wand. You can come in the back and see it if you want. Just you." He looked at Adelaide.

Adelaide nodded slowly. She looked at Kurt and then out to her friends in the corridor.

"Sure. Yes. Show me your magic wand." She gestured toward the back of the store. She tried to make eye contact with Darius, but there were too many people walking between the shop entrance and the bench where the others sat.

"Rad! Okay, come on." Kyber moved out from behind the counter and began to follow her. He paused and looked back toward the till. "Stay here," he ordered Kurt. "And don't steal anything, okay?"

Adelaide gave Kurt a sly smile as she followed Kyber through the door at the back of the store.

***

65

Darius craned his neck, trying to get a look through a throng of people into Rainy Day Games. They kept moving in such a way that his vision was blocked. When they finally parted, Darius caught a glimpse of Adelaide as she turned down the end of one of the aisles with Kyber and disappeared.

"Where's she going?" Darius walked toward the store.

"Easy," Tetsu called. "Don't blow her cover."

"She shouldn't be going somewhere alone with him," Darius fretted. "Kurt," he hissed.

Kurt waved Darius away.

Darius pursed his lips. He paced in front of the store.

"Sit down," Tetsu called over.

Darius ignored him and peered through the entrance into the store.

There was still no sign of Adelaide or Kyber.

Darius sighed. He knew he had to trust Adelaide. She'd been brave, braver than him, with the cyborg dog they'd found in the woods. He surveyed the mall corridor as he walked back to the bench.

More people walking. Some carried shopping bags.

Tetsu fished another donut out of the box. Sophie

looked bored.

Darius' eyes fell on a middle-aged man wearing a sport coat walking down the corridor. He recognized the man. He and Adelaide had seen him outside the dilapidated house on Hyacinth Street last month. It was Gary Stevens.

Darius sucked in his breath.

He glanced at the store, then back at Gary.

"We have to walk. Now," Darius hissed to Tetsu and Sophie.

Gary scanned the mall corridor.

"What?" Tetsu garbled through a mouth full of donut. Crumbs dropped onto the remaining donuts in the open box on his lap.

"Walk!" Darius hissed again. Sophie got to her feet and moved next to him.

"Hey kids," Gary called.

"Come on," Darius hissed at Tetsu again.

Gary strode down the corridor straight toward them.

"Kid, I've got a question for you."

Darius tried not to look at Gary. He cringed as he left Tetsu behind. With Sophie beside him, he turned and walked briskly down the hallway, and away from Rainy Day Games.

***

Adelaide felt weightless as she floated in the air. Her heart raced as she reached up with her fingers to touch the ceiling. She was in the back room of Rainy Day Games amidst boxes of excess inventory, floating several feet off the ground while Kyber pointed a metal staff, which was about five feet long, in her direction.

The device emitted a soft hum. It was made of a series of cylinders that could be twisted or turned, and Kyber had turned some of them before Adelaide had floated into the air. There were buttons midway down, strange metal buttons with symbols Adelaide couldn't decipher. Kyber's thumb was pressing one of them now, suspending her above the floor.

"Oh wow." Adelaide couldn't help but smile. She had thought it would take some convincing to see the magic staff, or that it would be a fake. That had not been the case. She supposed she should have been scared, but floating, which was the closest she'd been to flying, felt freeing. And after cyborg dogs and stitched together bodies, a teenage boy in the backroom of a game store didn't seem so scary. She also wanted answers, and that meant getting Kyber to trust her. "This is cool."

"Right? Technically it's a magic rod, not a magic wand. It's a family heirloom. I found it in my basement."

"So cool," Adelaide said. Floating in the air, it seemed magic was possible. She knew Kurt would claim the device just affected gravity somehow. "Did it belong to a great-grandparent?"

Kyber smiled. "I think it was my grandfather's." He lowered his voice and looked around, despite them being alone in the back room. "He worked at The Link. Cool, huh?"

"So cool. Do you have anything else like it?" Adelaide asked, worried this wasn't what they were looking for."

"Naw, this is it."

Adelaide breathed a small sigh of relief. "Does it do anything else?"

"Yeah, I mean, I guess." Kyber averted his gaze, but kept the rod pointed at her.

"You can tell me," Adelaide coaxed. "I think it's rad you're like a real-life magic-user."

"You do?" Kyber looked back at her.

"Uh huh. How do you get me down?"

"That's easy, but hey, can you grab that box while you're up there?" Kyber pointed.

"This one?" Adelaide reached for a box labelled, "Warhammer Fantasy Battle."

"Thanks, yeah," Kyber said as he lowered her gently to the ground. "Okay, well, I tried to open a portal to the lower realms, but it just made my friend vomit."

"That's grody. Did he help you clean it up?" Adelaide handed the box to Kyber.

He set the staff against the wall. It was made of segments of metal and it had several knobs and buttons on it. The end flared out.

"No." Kyber sighed. "It was gross. Come on, your friend will be waiting." A wave of panic crossed his face. "Oh shit, what if he thinks I was trying to do something pervy with you?"

"He might. You did talk about your rod a lot," Adelaide pointed out.

"Huh. You know, you're pretty cute. If you don't get all, you know, bitchy like girls do when they get to high school, you'll be a really cool chick. And the good kind of cool. Not like the lame posers."

"Thanks," Adelaide simply said. The idea of high school terrified her.

Kyber set the magic staff down inside the back room. The two of them stepped back out into the store.

Kyber was still carrying the box she had retrieved for him.

"Did you take anything?" Kyber eyed Kurt.

"No!" Kurt looked offended. He turned to Adelaide. "Are you okay?"

"I'm fine. Kyber lied. It wasn't a magic wand, it's a magic rod. It's pretty rad." She nodded at Kurt and turned back to Kyber. "So, how'd you use it to make the Kinkos disappear?"

Seven

The room was illuminated with flickering red and black candles placed in a perfect circle. Their soft glow was dim enough so the photocopiers along the perimeter of the store were almost unnoticeable. The metal security doors had been pulled shut and the mall itself was dark and still.

Half a dozen people in hooded robes took up their positions around the circle.

"This is going to work tonight, right?" Vernon Garva pressed.

"Oh yeah." Kyber nodded as he adjusted his grip on the magic rod. "Definitely going to work."

"Good." Vernon nodded as he looked around the Kinkos. "Tonight, Thantos will do my bidding."

Kyber swallowed. "Everyone in position?"

People looked at Kyber expectantly, and he began to chant. While the others knelt around the circle, their heads bowed low, Kyber walked the perimeter. He used his thumb to twist a few dials on the rod as he chanted.

Then, Kyber raised his voice to reach a crescendo and

waved the rod dramatically.

He called on Thantos.

The candles flared.

"Yes," Vernon hissed.

Kyber continued to chant as he paced the circle. He raised his voice again, and once more the candles flickered.

Kyber tried to cover his surprise.

"Yes! I can feel him," Vernon said with glee.

Kyber looked at the men positioned around the circle as he continued to chant. Then he raised his voice one final time and banged the end of the rod against the floor.

Everything went black.

Eight

"I—" Kyber glanced around nervously. "I just wanted to hang out, okay? I don't know where all the stuff disappeared to. It was supposed to be, like, roleplaying. I spoke pig Latin! But everything was gone." Kyber's eyes darted around the store.

"Everything was gone?" Kurt raised his eyebrows.

"Everything and *everyone*," Kyber whispered as he leaned in. His eyes were wild now. "I woke up and the mall was empty."

"Wasn't it after hours?" Adelaide frowned. "Hadn't people just gone home?"

"You don't understand." Kyber looked at the entrance of the store, then back at them. "The store was empty. The mall was deserted. Everyone was gone. *Everything.* I tried to recast the spell. I walked around the other way, like, I retraced my steps. Nothing happened. So, I went home because I didn't know what else to do. Hours had passed." His eyes bore into Adelaide's. "Hours," he whispered.

Adelaide shuddered.

"You just went home?" Kurt asked.

"What would *you* do?" He turned to Kurt. "I went home. Only the thing was, it wasn't my home." He looked haunted. "The furniture was my parents', sure. But it all felt wrong. Shadows stretched too far. The whole place was grey—greyer than it should have been. There were no pictures. No sign of my parents. Nothing. I was just alone."

Kurt and Adelaide exchanged glances.

Adelaide imagined her big old house devoid of people and fought the need to shudder again.

"What did you do?" Adelaide reached out and put her hand on Kyber's arm.

"I went to bed." He looked at her. His voice softened, the edge of panic fleeting. He sagged against the front counter. "I just went to bed. And when I woke up, my parents were there. Everything was normal."

"That explains the empty store, I guess." Adelaide looked at Kurt. "But I'm not sure why only the stuff in there went missing." She turned back to Kyber. "Did you close the store then?"

"I had to." His eyes pleaded. "What else was I supposed to do? It was all gone."

"So, where did the people and the stuff *go*?" Kurt asked.

"I don't know." Kyber looked down at his feet. "You guys should go. Unless you're buying that boxed set?" He looked at Kurt.

"I'll take your magic rod," Kurt said, looking Kyber square in the face.

Adelaide blinked in surprise and her hand fell from Kyber's arm.

"What? It's a family heirloom. Not a chance." Kyber took a step toward to back room.

"It's dangerous." Kurt looked toward the back of the store, then back at Kyber.

"It's not. It's …" Kyber trailed off. He averted their gaze.

"Wait. You left something out," Adelaide observed. "What else happened? Where did Vernon go?"

"He …" Kyber looked at them imploringly. "It wasn't my fault!"

Adelaide tilted her head and smiled softly. "It's okay, Kyber. You can tell us," she coaxed. There had to be more. "Who are we going to tell?"

Kyber looked between the two of them and then at the entrance.

Adelaide followed his gaze. There was no one else in the store, and she couldn't see the others. She wondered if they were on the nearby bench outside the store. "It's just us," she assured him.

Kyber dropped his voice to a whisper. "He came at me. He just kept yelling. I … I didn't know what to do. I didn't mean to." Kyber looked at Adelaide. He was frantic, pleading. "I didn't mean to."

"It's okay. Just tell us what happened." Adelaide took a step toward him and put her hand on his arm again. She needed to know what happened. She willed him, from the very core of her being, to explain what happened. Kyber took a deep breath.

"When, when it was all grey and everything was wrong, Vernon came back. He was angry. So angry. He had a gun." Kyber shivered and looked at the ground. "He pointed it at me. He yelled at me and told me to bring them all back—the people, the photocopiers—but I'd already tried." With his other hand, he grabbed Adelaide's wrist. She didn't move her hand off of his arm. "I'd already tried …"

"What happened next, Kyber?" Adelaide glanced at Kurt, who wore a worried expression. She hoped he wouldn't interrupt like Darius had earlier.

"He was a bad man. You have to believe me." Kyber looked at her imploringly. "He was laundering money in there. He didn't know I knew, but I did. And he had done something to one of the machines. It printed differently. It printed drugs onto the paper."

"Drugs?" Adelaide frowned.

"He was a drug dealer. Nothing about that place was what it seemed. It wasn't. He was a bad man." Kyber's eyes were wild now and his grip on Adelaide's wrist tightened.

"Kyber, tell me what happened next. He had a gun. He pointed it at you. What did you do?"

"I just pointed the staff." Kyber lowered his voice and closed his eyes. He looked as though he was trying to recall a dream or distant memory. "I just pointed the staff. Then he was …"

"He was what?" Kurt pushed.

Kyber tensed and swung to look at Kurt. His grip tightened even more on Adelaide's wrist.

Adelaide winced and shook her head at Kurt.

"Kyber, listen to me. Pay attention to me," Adelaide urged in her monotone voice. "He threatened you with a gun. What happened next?"

Kyber's gaze turned back to her and she felt him

relax the slightest bit. "He … it was like … you won't tell anyone?" Kyber pleaded.

"Kyber, I'm not the police. I'm a kid." Adelaide assured him. "Who would I tell?"

"Why do you even want to know?" he demanded. "How did you even know?"

"My mother worked there. She wasn't there that night, but I need to know what happened. I won't tell her. You're just telling me," Adelaide coaxed.

Kyber nodded slowly. "You promise?"

"Just tell me," Adelaide said softly.

"It was just supposed to be a game. I spoke pig Latin. He had the gun and I pointed the rod at him. I needed him not to hurt me." Kyber rambled. He took a deep breath, but he kept his gaze locked on Adelaide. "It was like a bolt of lightning hit him in the chest. It smelled like ozone, you know. You know that smell? And he … he was dead."

Adelaide nodded in the most reassuring fashion she could muster. She remembered that smell before a thunderstorm. It was like a burning wire: sweet and pungent.

"What did you do next?" she asked. Out of the corner of her eye she saw Kurt shuffle toward one of the aisles.

"I didn't know what to do," Kyber whispered. His eyes bore into hers.

"You were in the strange grey place. What did you do?" Adelaide urged.

"I—that's when I just closed the store. I left him there." A wave of guilt washed over Kyber's face. "He was dead. So dead. I left, and I went home. Everything was grey and still. When I woke up it was still wrong."

"Wrong how?" Adelaide asked. "I thought you said it was fine?"

Kurt was out of sight now. She hoped she was right and he was getting the staff.

"Not the first time," Kyber said. "The first time I woke up it was just … I don't know. Just wrong. I came back to the mall. The body was gone. And I, I closed the store. And I put up the sign. And I didn't want questions. I broke into the office," Kyber whispered.

"You changed the lease?" Adelaide asked impressed. "You forged that woman's signature?"

"It wasn't difficult," Kyber murmured. "I found something she'd signed. Her signature's simple enough. But everything was still wrong. And I went home and I, um …" Kyber looked at his feet. "I hid in my bed and fell asleep. And then when I woke up, everything was normal again." Kyber looked at Adelaide. His eyes were wide. "He wasn't a good person. I didn't mean to do it, but he wasn't a good person. He used the store as a front. He moved drugs and laundered money."

"I believe you," Adelaide said. Her stomach turned at the idea her mother had been employed by a criminal. Then it summersaulted at the idea she could have stayed late and fallen victim to whatever magic ritual or strange science Kyber had accidently conducted. She glanced over as Kurt emerged from one of the aisles with the rod. She had no idea what they were going to do with it, or who they would turn in such an item to. The Link? But what would the scientists there do with it?

"I believe you, Kyber," she said.

Kyber sighed with relief. Then he noticed Kurt and frowned.

"What are you doing?" Kyber demanded. "That's mine." He looked between the two of them confused.

"Kyber, it's a murder weapon." Adelaide's voice was even. She gave his arm a small squeeze. "You don't want a murder weapon here. You let us take it, and it'll be like none of this happened. You can just put it behind you."

"I don't want to go to jail ..." Kyber trailed off.

"Of course, you don't." Adelaide indicated Kurt should leave the store. "Of course, you don't. We have to go now, Kyber."

Kyber nodded slowly.

Nine

Darius and Sophie circled back to Rainy Day Games and found Tetsu on the bench nearby. He still had the box of donuts on his lap. His fingers were covered in sugar.

"I can't believe you ran away," Tetsu heckled.

"I can't believe you didn't." Darius felt guilty he'd left Tetsu behind, but he'd needed to draw Gary away from Adelaide. "Did he go in the game store?"

"No!" Tetsu's shoulders heaved with laughter. "He wanted to know where I got the donuts. He couldn't find his friend and figured he'd be there. And you ran away!" Tetsu chuckled. "Like a scared little baby."

Darius' fists balled up and he willed himself to take a take breath. He glanced back at Rainy Day Games and breathed a sigh of relief as Adelaide and Kurt exited the store.

Kurt carried a long metal rod with him.

"Hey, are you okay?" Darius stepped next to them.

"I'm fine." Adelaide nodded. "Thanks for your help, guys. I definitely can't get my mom's job back, but it sounds like it wasn't a great place for her to work. Great lead, Sophie."

Sophie beamed. "What happened?" Darius reached over and steadied the rod as Kurt adjusted his grip. "And what is that?"

"That a big enough rod for ya, or are you overcompensating, Kurt?" Tetsu laughed.

"Hey! Hey!" a voice called from inside the store. "I changed my mind! Get back here!"

Darius looked over at the entrance to Rainy Day Games where a red-headed teenager, presumably the Kyber they'd been looking for, beckoned Adelaide and Kurt.

"Well, crap!" Tetsu exclaimed. "Guess you aren't getting a giant rod after all."

"Run!" Kurt called.

Darius raised his eyebrows in surprise.

Kyber gritted his teeth and looked back at his cash register. Then he ran toward them.

Darius glanced at Adelaide. She nodded.

The two of them flanked Kurt and ran. They dodged and weaved through the crowd of mall patrons.

"Get back here! Thieves!" Kyber yelled from behind them.

"Was this the plan?" Darius asked. He skirted a woman with a stroller.

"Not exactly!" Kurt huffed.

"Get them!" Kyber called. "Security!"

A group of teenagers parted to let them through.

"Stick it to the man, man!" one of them called.

"Where are we going?" Darius asked, ignoring them. They were at the opposite end of the mall from his bike and he couldn't see Tetsu and Sophie.

"This way!" Adelaide steered them into the Kmart.

A woman with too much rouge on her cheeks and a dozen bags in hand leapt out of the way.

"Sorry!" Darius called back.

He cringed.

The woman had collided with the red bouncy ball vending machine.

"Come on!" Kurt hissed.

Adelaide slowed to a brisk walk.

Darius and Kurt followed suit.

Adelaide gave a brief nod to a woman with a small girl.

The woman averted her gaze and hurried her daughter forward.

The three of them were in the women's clothing

department now. There were racks of blouses, skirts and dresses all crammed together on racks arrayed on the thin brown carpet.

Adelaide glanced around and steered them off the discolored linoleum floor onto the carpet toward the racks of clothing.

There was a commotion toward the front of the store.

"Here." Adelaide scurried to a large round rack of women's blouses. She glanced around, parted the hangers and motioned for them to climb in.

"You first," Darius said as he nudged Kurt forward.

Darius took the metal rod and Kurt climbed in. Once Kurt was safely inside, Darius stepped over the lower silver bar and ducked under the bar the hangers hooked onto. He handed the rod back to Kurt and held his hand out for Adelaide.

He almost jumped as static discharged when they touched. She climbed into the rack and pulled the clothes back into place.

Ten

Darius, Kurt, and Adelaide huddled together between the articles on a women's clothing rack in Kmart. It was squishy, hot, and uncomfortable.

"How long do we wait?" Kurt whispered.

"A bit longer," Adelaide suggested. She wasn't sure how long Kyber would look around Kmart, but she was certain he'd be desperate to get his magic staff back.

"I can't believe he handed it over," Kurt marvelled. "I mean, you were convincing, Adelaide, it's just—"

"It's a magic staff?" Adelaide finished for him. She was as surprised as Kurt was and she couldn't figure out how she'd convinced Kyber or what they should do with the rod now.

"I don't know that it's magic," Kurt replied.

"Quiet guys," Darius urged.

They sat huddled together for another few minutes.

They all stiffened as footsteps drew closer.

The metal hangers scraped against the metal bar as some of the clothes were moved aside.

Adelaide sucked in her breath.

An older woman with greying hair pulled up into a bun gasped as she saw the lot of them. Her hand clutched her chest in fright.

"Sorry, ma'am," Darius said. He scrambled out of the clothing display and looked around. "Come on," he urged the others.

Adelaide didn't need to be told twice, and the woman looked like she was recovering from her scare. Adelaide grabbed Kurt's hand and pulled him out alongside her.

"You—you—" the woman started. "You can't hide in there!"

"We're very sorry," Adelaide said. "We have to go now."

She set a quick pace back toward the entrance of the store, scanning the area as she went. There were plenty of people, some of whom gave them a sideways glance as they carried a metal rod through the department store, but there was no sign of the red-headed game store clerk.

"Where do you think the others are?" Kurt asked as they stepped out into the mall corridor.

"Food court maybe?" Darius suggested. "Tetsu seems to like it there."

Adelaide laughed loudly, from deep down in her belly.

Darius and Kurt both turned and stared at her.

She clapped her hand over her mouth as other mall patrons turned to see what the noise was.

Adelaide wasn't sure what Darius had said was even that funny, but the laugh had bubbled out, the stress of the afternoon catching up with her.

She willed herself to take a deep breath, but she bellowed another laugh instead.

"Are you okay?" Kurt asked.

Adelaide nodded as they pressed their way through the mall corridor.

People were still watching.

She took short quick breaths and reminded herself there was nothing funny about the situation at all. Adelaide managed one longer deeper breath and the urge to laugh subsided.

"I'm okay now," Adelaide said.

"You were laughing," Darius said dumbly. He had a look of bewilderment on his face.

"I suppose I was. I'm not sure what came over me," Adelaide said. In truth, it had felt good to laugh that hard, but Adelaide knew they didn't need any more attention on them, or the giant metal staff they were carrying through the mall.

She led the three of them toward the food court, then paused and changed course.

"Where are we going?" Darius asked.

"The bike rack. We ran off in a hurry. I bet they're waiting outside."

"Good thinking," Darius agreed.

Just as Adelaide predicted, Sophie and Tetsu loitered near the bike rack.

"About time. It's cold out here!" Tetsu complained.

"I can't believe you guys were chased in the mall. This is so embarrassing," Sophie added.

"Thanks for waiting for us," Adelaide replied.

"My bike is on the other side of the mall," Darius admitted.

Tetsu opened his mouth to say something, but Adelaide spoke first.

"We'll walk you over there," she said.

Darius took the rod from Kurt as he, and the others, collected their bikes.

***

The quintet made their way around the outside of the mall toward Darius' bike.

"So, what is going on?" Sophie asked. "My lead was really good, right? Come on, spill it."

"It sounds like Kinkos was into some shady business practices," Kurt said. "Kyber thinks Vernon used the place to launder money."

"Launder money?" Sophie asked. She turned to Tetsu expectantly.

"What? You just assume I know?" Tetsu balked.

"It's cleaning dirty money, like crime money, drug money, that sort of thing," Kurt explained. "Making it able to be used without people asking questions. It's complicated to do properly, I think. I've only read about it in books." He glanced at Tetsu.

"Stop that," Tetsu warned.

Darius looked between them all, wondering what was going on.

"Anyway," Adelaide cut in. "I guess Kinkos was a front and that's why their head office didn't think there was a branch here."

"But that wasn't enough." Kurt shook his head. "He had Kyber try to summon some sort of creature to do his bidding, but Kyber didn't do it properly. The guy—Vernon, right?"

Adelaide nodded.

"He freaked out when the stuff in the store, and the other people, disappeared," Kurt continued.

Darius was sure there was something the two of them weren't saying, but he just nodded.

"So, what's that thing?" Tetsu pointed at the rod.

"It's the magic rod Kyber used to make an entire store and half a dozen people disappear. He also used it to defend himself against Vernon," Adelaide said in a matter-of-fact tone.

"I'm still not sure it's magic." Kurt shook his head. "I don't believe in magic. There must be some sort of scientific explanation."

"Magic or not, it isn't a normal hunk of metal," Adelaide replied. "He made people disappear with it."

"I can see why he didn't want to give it up. What did you do? Snatch it and run?" Tetsu asked. There was a note of awe in his voice.

"No," Adelaide smiled at Kurt. "Kurt said he was taking it. He told Kyber he wasn't allowed to keep it as it was too dangerous."

"*You* just told him and he said *yes*?" Tetsu raised his eyebrows.

"I told him, and then Adelaide told him. So, we took it. Then I guess he changed his mind." Kurt gave a tight smile. "Anyway, we have it now."

"The security guard—was he in on the drugs and money laundering then?" Darius asked.

"Of course, he was!" Tetsu exclaimed. "He had to be in on all of it."

Darius fought the urge to roll his eyes.

"Come on!" Tetsu said. "You don't think he'd notice a bunch of people in robes summoning a demon or whatever it was? He was totally in on it. I bet they paid him to keep quiet."

"What?" Darius asked.

"Keep up," Tetsu said snapping his fingers. "Sophie said the girls at Bootlegger saw Kyber in a 'hooded dress thing.' That's a robe. And some 'creature to do his bidding' is a demon or somethin'." Tetsu shook his head and looked disapprovingly at Darius.

Darius gritted his teeth.

"Do we tell someone?" Sophie asked.

"That we think the security guard is probably somehow involved in drugs and money laundering when all the evidence is gone?" Kurt asked skeptically. "The police would have a lot of questions for us, including why we think that."

Darius thought of the agents and shivered.

"Let's just get out of here," Sophie said.

"Yeah," Tetsu agreed. "Besides, it's always good to know a dirty cop. Or, you know, mall security guard."

"What?" Darius turned and frowned at Tetsu.

"You heard me."

Darius just shook his head.

"Just ignore him," Kurt mumbled. "He likes to talk a big game."

They reached Darius' bike. Darius moved the numbers on the pad until they matched the combination. He snapped the lock open and freed his bike. He was the only one of them with a bike lock, and he waited for Tetsu to comment.

Tetsu was surprisingly quiet, and Darius wondered if the donuts he'd purchased earlier had bought him some goodwill. He wondered how long it would last.

Kurt fumbled with the rod as he climbed onto his bike.

"Let me do it, Kurt," Adelaide offered.

Kurt handed it over, and Adelaide took the rod and balanced it alongside her. One end of it balanced on the basket affixed to the back of her bike while the other end rested on the handle bars.

They all climbed on their bikes and started to pedal out of the parking lot.

"Maybe we should tell the police about Vernon," Kurt suggested.

"Tell them what?" Adelaide asked. "There's a guy who sold drugs, but disappeared into somewhere and he was murdered by a magic rod. We'd sound crazy. There isn't really anything anyone can do now, other than make sure that thing doesn't do any more damage."

They all rode in silence.

"What will you do with that thing?" Darius asked as they reached the road.

"I'll try to take it apart and see how it works," Kurt said.

"That sounds like a terrible idea," Sophie cut in.

"I dunno. Maybe he'll make a huge pile of money appear," Tetsu said with a grin.

"Doubtful. You could get hurt, Kurt!" Sophie exclaimed.

Adelaide frowned. Sophie was right. "We need to be careful with it." Adelaide adjusted her grip on the rod, careful not to push any of the buttons. "We could just keep it in my basement. No one ever goes down there."

"Well, I guess I'll see you guys later," Darius said as they reached the road where he had to turn and head back to his neighbourhood. He often wished he lived closer to them.

"Yeah. See ya!" Tetsu said without a backward glance.

"Bye, Darius. Thanks for the Orange Julius." Sophie stopped her bike and smiled at him.

"Thanks, Darius," Kurt said as he pulled up his bike as well.

Adelaide pulled her bike up next to Darius'.

"Thanks for your help, Darius. We couldn't have done it without you." Adelaide gave a small smile. "See you at school tomorrow."

There was so much Darius wanted to say, about how magnificent her laugh was, or how he wanted to make her laugh every day for the rest of his life, or how she was the bravest and most amazing person he'd ever met.

Instead, he said, "See you then."

Adelaide nodded, turned, and followed her friends down the road.

Part Two

One

The last of the leaves had fallen from the trees and smoke twisted out of the chimneys of nearby houses. Adelaide stepped out of her house. The cold air nipped at her cheeks. She breathed in the smell of fall: rotting leaves, chimney smoke, and crisp autumnal air.

"Mornin'," Tetsu said as Adelaide pulled the front door closed behind her. He had knocked once, then leaned against the house while he waited for her. Now that she was outside, he peeled himself off the wall.

"Morning, Tetsu," Adelaide replied. She locked the door and shouldered her backpack.

"Here." Tetsu slipped a few bunched-up bills into Adelaide's hand.

"What is this?" Adelaide asked with a frown.

Tetsu rolled his eyes. "It's money."

"I can see that," Adelaide said with sigh. "Why did you hand me money?"

"Look, don't make this a big thing. I just noticed you haven't had as much cereal around. I like cereal. So just take it," Tetsu said. He fell in step with her as they made their way off the front porch toward the street.

"I can't—"

"Yeah, you can." Tetsu nodded toward a grey Ford Taurus parked in the driveway. "Whose car is that?"

Adelaide shrugged. "I didn't catch his name."

Earlier that month, Belinda, Adelaide's mother, had lost her job at a copy centre quite suddenly. And then, a week and a half ago, while she was still reeling from the job loss, Belinda's boyfriend Rico had broken up with her.

Rico, who had a disturbing habit of blinking far more than any person should, had shown up when he felt like it and spent most of the night making loud noises with Belinda in her bedroom.

Rico said Belinda was smothering him and he needed space but, despite how needy her mother could be, Adelaide didn't think that was the whole reason for the breakup.

Adelaide didn't miss his presence, even if she'd spent two nights consoling her mother while she slept in Adelaide's bedroom. For the last week or so Belinda had found an assortment of men to console her instead.

"Your mom has had a lot of people over lately," Tetsu observed. When Adelaide didn't respond, he continued. "I just mean, it kind of makes her look like, well, you know, a slut."

Adelaide stopped walking. She turned and looked at him. Her face was solemn.

It took a moment for Tetsu to realize she'd stopped. He glanced back at her and winced.

Adelaide pursed her lips. She knew what some people said about her mother. She just didn't think Tetsu would be one of them.

"We don't choose our parents, Tetsu Nomura," Adelaide said pointedly. She resumed walking, but she refused to look at him.

"I—"

"I'm not talking about it." Adelaide turned to look at the Katillion house as Sophie emerged. It wasn't often she was out before Kurt.

Sophie sighed as she walked toward them. "This is for you," Sophie grumbled as she thrust a paper bag at Adelaide. "My mom asked me to give it to you."

"Thanks, Sophie," Adelaide said.

Tetsu, who had often made comments in the past about how Sheila Katillion never made lunches for him, was remarkably quiet. Adelaide's stomach twisted at the realization her friends could see how much she and her mother were struggling.

Adelaide was ripped from her thoughts as Kurt stepped out of the Zillman house next door to Sophie's. His head was down, his reddish-brown hair hanging forward as if to cover his face. Despite his feeble efforts, the livid purple bruise around his right eye was immediately evident.

"What happened to you?" Sophie gasped.

"I fell out of bed," Kurt mumbled. "Can we go?"

Tetsu looked between Kurt and the house. He raised his eyebrows and nodded. "Sure, yeah."

"Let's go, guys," Adelaide said. She gave Kurt a small, encouraging smile.

She might be hungry, but Kurt had far bigger problems.

***

Darius waited eagerly as the familiar bus pulled up outside the school. He watched as the doors opened and knew Adelaide would be one of the first people off the bus.

He grinned as she descended the stairs.

She wore her usual wrist cuff, and her long dark

hair hung past at her shoulders. Her eyes seemed to sparkle just a little bit as they fell on him. He hoped it wasn't his imagination.

Darius moved toward her as other students filed off the bus behind her. Then he recoiled in shock at the sight of Kurt. Darius glanced at the others for any indication of what might have happened. Sophie and Tetsu avoided his gaze. Adelaide just shook her head softly.

"Kurt, are you all right?"

"I'm fine. I fell out of bed," Kurt replied without meeting Darius' gaze.

"Kurt! Come on," Darius said with a grimace. "There's no way you did that falling out of bed. You can tell me." Kurt still refused to meet Darius' gaze.

"I fell out of bed," he repeated.

Darius looked around the others. Tetsu and Sophie still wouldn't look at him. Kurt looked like he wanted to be anywhere but there. Adelaide shook her solemn face again, imploring him to leave it alone.

He had no idea why they weren't more concerned or why, after all they'd been through together, they weren't being honest with him.

"Fine," Darius said.

As they stood in silence, waiting for the bell to ring,

Darius wondered if Mr. McKenzie would have any more luck getting to the truth of the matter.

A few minutes later, the students of James Morrison Elementary trundled off to their classrooms, hung their coats and backpack on hooks in the cloakrooms and took their seats. Darius had his second shock of the day when he saw Mr. McKenzie enter the classroom dressed in a bright yellow Funshine Bear costume.

"He dresses up every day of the week leading up to Halloween," Adelaide explained.

"Ah," Darius said. None of the teachers at Wiltshire Preparatory Academy in Boston had ever dressed up for Halloween. He liked Mr. McKenzie even more now, and he crossed his fingers his favourite teacher could help his friend.

Mr. McKenzie smiled at the students as they filed to their desks, but a shadow crossed his face when his eyes fell on Kurt.

Mr. McKenzie called Kurt up to his desk at the front of the classroom, and Kurt went, if a bit reluctantly.

Darius leaned forward and squinted as if doing so might let him glean a little of the conversation.

The hum of his classmate's chatter made it impossible.

"What happened?" Darius asked as he turned to Adelaide. "Was it Tetsu?"

"What?" Adelaide asked, confused. She had been watching Kurt and Mr. McKenzie as well, but she turned to face Darius. "Tetsu?"

"What?" Tetsu asked from her other side.

Darius shifted his gaze between them. He knew accusing Tetsu directly would ruin any progress he had made with Adelaide's best friend.

"I was asking what you two knew about what happened to Kurt," Darius replied instead. He looked at Adelaide and hoped she would go along with it.

"It ain't any of your business," Tetsu said flatly and turned back to face the front of the classroom.

"He's my friend," Darius argued.

Tetsu ignored him.

"Darius, I know he's your friend. He's our friend, too. It's just that ..." Adelaide's eyes flicked back over to Kurt. She paused. "It's just that there isn't anything we can do that won't make it worse."

"That doesn't make sense," Darius argued. "Who did that to him? We'll just report whoever bullied him to the school. Or *I'll* talk to them."

Darius felt anger rumble inside of him. People like

Kurt didn't deserve to be treated like this. He balled up his fists, his nails digging into his palms.

Mr. McKenzie looked at Kurt intently, said something, and then gave a warm smile.

Kurt nodded and turned to walk back to his desk.

"Darius," Adelaide said gently. She leaned over closer to him. Her eyes searched his face imploringly. Her voice was quieter than usual now, underscored with melancholy. "It's not another kid. It's his dad. And if anyone gets involved, it'll get worse. Or he'll get taken away and we'll never see him again. So please, please just leave it."

Two

The friends of Pine Street gathered in the rec room at Sophie's, a place they often referred to as the Hideout. "Suffragette City" by David Bowie played in the background.

Adelaide fidgeted with a strand of orange shag carpet. She couldn't quite twist it around her finger.

Sophie flicked through the pages of the latest *Teen Beat* magazine.

There was a rap at the door before it opened.

Butterflies fluttered in Adelaide's stomach as she looked up in anticipation. A hint of a smile crossed her lips as Sophie's older brother, Andy, stepped into the room. He had warm brown eyes and a mop of blond hair that reminded Adelaide of a halo. He wore jeans and a pale blue shirt.

"Hey guys," Andy said. "Mom asked me to,"—his voice went up an octave and he coughed—"to bring these down." He nodded toward the plate he carried in one hand, piled with grilled cheese sandwiches. He had something, a record perhaps, tucked under this arm.

Adelaide tried to see what it was without drawing attention to herself.

"Oh my gawd. You are such a loser," Sophie moaned as she flicked another page of the magazine. "Just put them on the table or something."

Andy looked over toward Adelaide.

Their eyes met and Adelaide's breath caught in her throat. She felt her cheeks redden and she looked away.

Andy stepped toward Adelaide and held the plate out to her.

She gingerly took a hot, golden sandwich off the plate. "Thanks," she said quietly.

"You're welcome," Andy squeaked as he stepped back toward the wooden coffee table and set down the plate.

"Mind if I put on a record?" he asked as he moved next to her.

Adelaide looked up and realized Andy was talking to her.

"There's already music on," Sophie pointed out.

Andy ignored her.

"Okay." Adelaide nodded, also ignoring Sophie. Her heart fluttered as he lowered himself to the ground and sat cross-legged next to her.

Sophie groaned and flicked another page of her magazine. Tetsu was busy devouring the grilled cheese sandwiches, and Kurt seemed engrossed in *The Return of the King*.

"I borrowed this from a friend. I haven't listened to it yet," Andy said as he passed her the copy of *Slippery When Wet*. His voice went up another octave and his face reddened. "Have you heard it?"

Adelaide shook her head. She had the urge to reach over and take his hand, but she twisted her fingers into the orange shag instead.

"Are you going to dress up for Halloween?" Adelaide asked. "Or is that"—she paused looking for the right words—"do you not do that in high school?"

"I don't really know if people do it. I think some people are, and some aren't. I don't know if I will." Andy slipped the record out of the sleeve and placed it on the turntable.

Adelaide watched as Andy moved the tone arm and set the stylus atop the record. She closed her eyes as the needle scratched the disc. Adelaide smiled at the static popping sound. She could feel the smile spread across her face. The sound of a revving guitar broke the static and

Adelaide opened her eyes.

Andy smiled at her.

Adelaide felt her cheeks redden.

"Hey, Andy!" Tetsu called from his seat in the beanbag chair. He was holding the whole plate of sandwiches now. "What are the girls in high school like?"

Adelaide tucked her hair behind her ear and looked down at the floor. She imagined a lot of the girls in high school were interested in Andy. He was only in eighth grade, but he had managed to secure a spot as a backup quarterback on the junior varsity football team.

"Fine?" Andy squeaked.

"I'm Andy!" Sophie squawked.

"Hey!" Andy frowned as a crumpled-up piece of paper hit him in the arm.

"Get out of here *loser*."

Adelaide held her breath. She'd been invited to dinner, but dinner wasn't enough time with Andy. She didn't want him to go.

"This isn't your room, Sophie. I can be in here if I want," Andy argued. "I want to use the record player."

"Then shut up about it," Sophie moaned.

Adelaide reached over and turned the knob on the speaker. The music increased in volume. Andy lifted his head back and shook his hair out of his face. Their eyes met and they both smiled.

***

The Katillion family sat around the large wooden dining room table. Andy took a sip of water and tried not to stare at Adelaide. He could feel Sophie watching him. His mother, Sheila, had tried her hand at a new recipe she'd found in *Women's Weekly* and the room smelled of Italian spices, and tomato sauce.

"This is great, Mom," Andy said after he swallowed another forkful.

"Do you think so?" Sheila fussed. "I mean, I like it, but you like it? Chicken cacciatore. It sounds so decadent."

"I like it," Andy assured her.

"How about you, sweetie?" Sheila asked Adelaide.

"I'm sorry to tell you I don't, Mrs. Katillion," Adelaide said, her voice flat and impassive.

Andy looked over surprised.

Adelaide's face was as solemn as ever.

"I'm sorry, sweetie." Sheila looked as though she'd been smacked. "I—"

111

"I don't like it, Mrs. Katillion. I love it." Adelaide scooped up another forkful. There was a twinkle in her eye as she looked back at Sheila.

Jack Katillion, Andy and Sophie's father, burst out laughing, then choked on his food. He coughed once, thumping himself in the chest with his fist, and resumed laughing.

Andy chuckled.

Adelaide's cheeks flushed the slightest bit.

Sheila smiled, and the smile quickly deepened until she was grinning.

"It wasn't that funny," Sophie sulked.

A small smile spread across Adelaide's face.

Andy wondered if Adelaide ever made jokes like that in the Hideout. He loved her smile, her soothing voice and her taste in music. He was surprised to discover that he loved her sense of humour as well.

"You had me there," Sheila said, amused. She reached over and clapped Jack on the back. "I'm glad you like it, Adelaide."

"That was a good one!" Jack spluttered. "Well played, Adelaide."

Sophie rolled her eyes. "Did you get my costume, Mom?"

"Yes, Sophie-dear. I found a witch costume just like you asked for. It looks very authentic," Sheila assured her.

"Whew. Good. And it's from that new place, right?" Sophie checked.

"Yes, Dizzy Izzy's Costume Emporium. They had quite a good selection. Strange man, but excellent costumes."

"Strange how?" Jack asked interested. "He hit on you, didn't he?" He chuckled. "You're an attractive woman, Sheila. I'm not surprised."

Sophie rolled her eyes at her father.

Sheila smiled, amused. "Thank you, dear. He did not, in fact, 'hit on me' as you say. He was just, odd. I can't put my finger on it." A shadow crossed her face, but then she blinked and it was gone.

Andy wondered if he had imagined it.

"Andy, are you sure you don't want one?" Sheila asked.

"I am," Andy replied. "I'll make do with what I have. Making your own costume is more fun, anyway. If I decide to dress up."

He cast a glance at Adelaide. She wasn't looking at him, but she seemed to be listening carefully.

"Suit yourself," Sophie said. "But I'm not risking

some lame costume."

"You might not dress up, Andy?" Jack asked, astounded. "But it's fun. I'm dressing up." He turned to Sheila. "I am, right? You got us costumes as well?"

Sheila smiled and shook her head in amusement. "Yes, Jack."

"Right. There, you see?" Jack tried to convince Andy.

"I dunno, Dad. I'll probably dress up," Andy replied. He liked the idea of dressing up, he just wasn't set on an idea yet. And he didn't want to be one of the only people at school in a costume.

"Do you have a plan, sweetie?" Sheila asked Adelaide carefully. "If you need any help …"

"Thank you, Mrs. Katillion. Really. I've got my costume sorted out, though," Adelaide assured her.

Andy wanted to ask what it was, but before he could open his mouth, Sophie cut in.

"Mr. Zillman hurt Kurt again."

Jack and Sheila shared a look.

"Can't you go talk to him or something?"

Andy had seen Kurt's black eye in the Hideout this afternoon. Kurt had done a great job of trying to hide his face behind his book, but eventually he had lowered it. Andy hadn't said anything. He had just given him the friendliest and most sympathetic smile he could muster. Mr. Zillman had always scared Andy. Sometimes, when he was lying in bed trying to fall asleep, he could hear Mr. Zillman yelling next door.

"Sophie-dear," Sheila started. "We want to, it's just—"

"It's just that sometimes interfering can make it worse," Jack finished.

"So, you won't do anything?" Sophie asked.

Adelaide looked like she was listening even more intently now.

"I, we," Jack corrected himself, "will talk about it." He looked at Sheila, who nodded.

Sophie did not look satisfied, but she nodded and turned her attention back to her dinner.

Nothing about Gus Zillman sat right with Andy, and he wished he could think of something to do about it. Surely there had to be someone who could help.

The rest of the meal passed uneventfully.

Jack, who was an accountant, talked at length about the poor state of the economy.

Jack loved his job, but Andy suspected tonight's conversation was also meant to fill the air. He tuned in and out and hoped he would not be as obsessed with something as boring as finance and economics when he became an adult.

Every now and then, Andy stole a look at Adelaide, who sat up straight and solemn-faced as ever, as she ate her dinner.

"Thank you for dinner, Mrs. Katillion, Mr. Katillion. It was very good. I can help with the dishes," Adelaide offered as everyone finished.

"That's lovely. Thanks sweetie," Sheila beamed at her.

"I've got homework, so …" Sophie stood up and scurried out of the dining room with her empty plate.

Andy heard her set it on the kitchen counter.

"I'd be happy to help," Andy said. His voice squeaked again and he tried not to grimace. Some of the other boys at school had the same problem, but none of their breaking voices were as pronounced as his was.

His father's voice was deep, and Andy suspected that was part of it.

"Thanks, you two," Jack said. He stood and picked up his plate as well as Sheila's. "I suppose that means you and I have a little free time?" He smiled slyly at Sheila.

"Jack!" Sheila swatted him, but smiled playfully.

Andy flushed. He gathered his plate and reached for Adelaide's, but she had already collected it.

She gave him a kind glance.

Jack dropped his plates in the kitchen.

"Andy, sweetie. Your father and I are going for a walk. You'll walk Adelaide home, won't you?" Sheila asked.

"Of course, Mom," Andy said. The time spent walking Adelaide home was the highlight of his day.

"Wonderful. Thanks again for coming over, sweetie," Sheila said to Adelaide.

"Thank you for having me."

"Did you want to wash or dry?" Andy asked as he plugged the sink, added a squirt of dish soap, and turned on the hot water.

"I don't mind either," Adelaide replied. "Which do you prefer?"

Andy had heard some kids once say that Adelaide's voice was devoid of emotion, but it always made his heart beat faster. In a good way.

"I could—" Andy grimaced as his voice faltered again. He coughed and looked at the kitchen floor embarrassed. "I could wash, and if you don't know where something goes—"

"I'll ask you." A hint of a smile played on her lips.

"Okay," Andy replied as he turned off the tap.

The two worked in an awkward yet comfortable silence with only the occasional question from Adelaide about where something went. She was familiar with the kitchen.

"We make a great team," Andy said.

The last of the water slurped down the drain.

Adelaide hung the tea towel over the oven door handle and nodded.

"You'll walk me home?" she asked.

"I said I would," Andy replied.

They slipped on their shoes and coats and Adelaide slung her backpack over her shoulder. He held the door open for her.

Andy walked as slowly as he thought he could get away with, and Adelaide kept pace.

"This school year is good?" Andy asked.

"It's fine," Adelaide said. She looked over at him. "You?"

Andy nodded. "Sophie says you, uh, have a boyfriend. Darius?" Andy blurted.

"We aren't boyfriend and girlfriend."

"Oh." Andy breathed a sigh of relief.

"Do you have a girlfriend?" Adelaide asked.

"Me? No." Andy thought of the girls at school and shuddered. He couldn't imagine spending a prolonged period of time with any of them. "No. I'm too busy for a girlfriend. I've got school. And homework. And work. I don't just mow our lawn," Andy rambled as he gestured at the lawn. He didn't know how to stop talking. "I mow other people's lawns now, too. I've saved up a bunch of money. Three hundred and fifty dollars."

"What are you going to do with it?" Adelaide asked.

"College, maybe? I'm not really sure," Andy admitted.

"So, you can be a private investigator."

Andy turned and looked at her as they walked. He wondered how she knew that.

"Your mom mentioned it last month, when we were in the minivan," Adelaide explained.

Andy recalled the day. He had asked if he could go with his mom to pick up Sophie from volleyball practice. He had hoped Adelaide might be there. And she had been.

It surprised him she had remembered that.

"Yeah, um, that. Or, well, I'd really like to be Indiana Jones or James Bond," Andy admitted. He waited

119

for her laugh at him.

Her face remained solemn.

"I could see that. It might be kind of difficult to raid tombs now. Maybe James Bond?"

Andy's heart skipped a beat.

Adelaide gestured at her house. "This is me."

"So it is," Andy said as he looked up at her house. It was at the very end of the street, visible as soon as one turned onto Pine Street. The sight of it always made Andy feel like he was home.

"Thanks for walking me back up the street."

"Any time," Andy said. He pressed his lips together and then smiled. "I'll wait here until you get in okay."

Adelaide nodded, then gave him a shy smile. She turned and walked up the front steps and into the house.

Andy sighed. He replayed the conversation in his head as he walked home and grimaced when he realized he implied he didn't want a girlfriend.

Three

Early morning rays of light trickled in through the large windows on the main floor. It was a sad, cold light, the kind that filtered through the windows in late October.

Adelaide imagined it would be a dreary winter. She didn't mind too much. She enjoyed the summer, but the cold weather didn't bother her as much as it bothered her friends. Adelaide often wondered if it was the drafty house she was used to, or if it was something she could attribute to her last name: Winter.

Matt, who also lived on Pine Street, was friends with Andy. Adelaide had once overheard them talking about her grandmother. Matt had sworn his mother had been scared of the creepy, reclusive Winter Witch in her ancient haunted house. Andy had laughed and told him the house was old, but not haunted. Matt had said there was something weird about the entire family. Andy had told him to "can it" and insisted that even if Adelaide's grandmother had been a bit odd, there was nothing weird about Adelaide Winter or her mother.

Adelaide's insides warmed at the memory.

It was almost time to leave for school.

Adelaide had cobbled together a lunch and eaten a spoonful of peanut butter for breakfast. She hadn't wanted to take Tetsu's money yesterday, but she had it now. She promised herself she would bike up to Rutledge's, the nearby convenience store, after school to restock some staples in the pantry.

There was a familiar knock at the front door.

Adelaide was still frustrated with Tetsu after yesterday's comment about her mother's promiscuity, but she liked the routine of him coming to meet her each morning. She hadn't liked their fight earlier this year and she wondered what, if anything, she should say to him now.

Adelaide shouldered her bag, walked out of the kitchen, and slipped her shoes on.

When she opened the front door, Tetsu stood there with a confused expression on his face.

"Hey, should he be …?" Tetsu trailed off and pointed to the deck where Waylon lay curled up outside. His back was pressed against the wall and he used one arm as a pillow while the other hugged his cowboy hat like a stuffed teddy bear.

Adelaide guessed Waylon was in his early twenties, but she had never asked. He was tall with sandy brown hair. Even under the grey days of Olympic Vista, his skin was tanned. Adelaide often wondered if all his years in Texas had left him permanently bronzed. He was broad shouldered and muscular, another side-effect of his time on the range.

"No," Adelaide said with a sigh. "Waylon, Waylon."

Adelaide walked over, bent down, and squeezed his shoulder.

"What's that?" Waylon yawned.

"You were asleep on the porch, Waylon," Adelaide pointed out.

"I s'pose I was," Waylon drawled in his Texan accent. He clamoured to his feet. "Left my keys at work."

Waylon's beat up red truck was parked in front of the house.

"How'd you get home?" Tetsu asked.

"That old thing doesn't need a key. Just shove a screw driver in the ignition," Waylon explained. "Didn't want to wake anyone up when I got in so early." He picked up his cowboy hat off the porch.

"Thanks, Waylon," Adelaide said with a note on concern. "I appreciate it, but you shouldn't have to sleep out here."

"Yeah, stay in your truck next time." Tetsu scoffed.

"Or just wake me up," Adelaide said. She frowned at Tetsu.

"Mighty kind of ya, little miss." Waylon tipped his hat to her before he placed it on his head. "Well, if you'll excuse me, I'll shower off the club and get some shut eye." Waylon's cowboy boots clicked on the porch as he strolled to the front door. "Have a good day at school y'all!"

"Thanks, Waylon." Adelaide waved goodbye and she and Tetsu descended the front steps and set off down the street.

"So, this Halloween party Darius is having, I was thinking, maybe we should go together?" Tetsu asked.

"Together? Like we should carpool?" Adelaide asked. Late last week Darius had suggested the two of them throw a Halloween party. Typically, she would have gone trick-or-treating and hoped for mini boxes of raisins to supplement her lunch with, but she rather liked the idea of hosting a party with Darius again. "I guess we could. I thought I should probably go early to setup, though. I am a co-host."

"Right, no, of course." Tetsu looked down at his feet and kicked a stray pebble on the road. "That makes sense."

Adelaide's eyebrows pinched together in confusion. She thought she might have offended him, but she was still upset about yesterday.

"Hey guys," Kurt said as he came out of the house. His black eye did not look any better today.

Adelaide looked toward his house, then back at him. "Hi Kurt," she said.

Sophie joined them and the four of them walked to the bus stop.

"Are there any songs any of you really want to hear at the party?" Adelaide asked. "I haven't finished the mixed tape yet."

"Ooh! Yes! You should put on 'Walk Like an Egyptian!'" Sophie exclaimed.

"I could try to do that," Adelaide replied. She wondered if she could record a clean enough copy off the radio that it wouldn't sound out of place on tape.

"I think Adelaide means from albums she has access to," Kurt said.

"Oh. Whatever then." Sophie sulked.

"I'll see what I can do, Sophie," Adelaide promised. "Maybe some Bananarama" She turned to the others. "How about you, Kurt?"

"You make great mixed tapes, Adelaide. Whatever

you put on will be fine," Kurt assured her.

"Well, I'd like to hear—"

"She didn't ask you, Tetsu," Sophie spat.

"Someone's crabby," Tetsu observed.

"Maybe I just don't like how you get. You aren't the boss, you know," Sophie said.

Tetsu looked wounded.

There was a trio of kids from Tetsu's street waiting for the bus that looked like they were listening intently.

Adelaide grimaced. She knew how much Tetsu liked to think he was the boss. She breathed a sigh of relief as she spotted the bus coming down the road toward them.

The bus pulled up and opened its doors to reveal the usual rumble of chatter interspersed with the occasional yell, squeal, or roar of laughter.

The trio boarded the bus first, then Sophie, followed by Kurt.

"Sophie! Sophie!" Julie called. She sat several rows behind where Adelaide always sat. "Come *on*, Sophie!" Julie's eyes bulged as if they'd burst with whatever juicy bit of gossip she was desperate to share.

"I thought she didn't want you to sit with her anymore?" Tetsu asked Sophie as he climbed aboard.

Sophie ignored Julie and slipped into the second

bench from the front where Kurt often sat.

"Come on, Sophie! I have huge news and I *have* to share!" Julie called over the other voices.

Kurt slid into the seat next to Sophie.

The front of the bus was the quietest place and Adelaide slipped into her usual seat just behind the stairwell. Tetsu had given up trying to convince her to move toward the back with the other older kids. He slid into the seat next to Adelaide.

The bus doors closed.

Adelaide turned to look at her friends in the seat behind her. She could see Julie several rows back.

"Sophie, come *on*." Julie's eyes flicked to Kurt, then back to Sophie.

Sophie kept her head facing forward.

Kurt craned his neck, but then turned back in his seat to face the others. "Don't you want to know what she has to say?" Kurt asked Sophie.

Julie's eyes almost bore holes into the back of Sophie's skull.

"I don't really care," Sophie declared as the bus pulled away from the curb.

Adelaide could tell nothing could be further from the truth.

***

Darius looked up as Davia entered the kitchen.

She wore a striped tennis shirt paired with an acid wash micro-mini jean skirt and a thick layer of colourful powder caked her eyelids.

Darius took a bite of his bran muffin and waited for his father to notice. He was still reeling from yesterday and could not understand how any parent could hurt their child the way Kurt's dad had hurt Kurt. Drew was a strict, no-nonsense man. Darius was not sure he liked his father very much. Sometimes he wasn't sure if he even loved him. But he didn't hate him. And he could never imagine his father lifting a hand to hit him or anyone else.

"So, your costumes are all set. I'm not sure if I told you that already," Miranda said.

"Why do they need costumes?" Drew looked up from his paper.

"It's almost Halloween, Daddy," Davia replied.

Drew almost spat out his coffee. "What are you wearing?"

"Makeup," Davia replied innocently.

"Too much of it. What is that? The whole package? Go wash it off," Drew ordered. He looked over at

Miranda. "And the children are too old to trick-or-treat now." He looked back down at his paper.

On any other day, the whole interaction would have amused Darius. He might have even needed to cover his mouth to hide a chuckle, but he was still too upset about Kurt.

"Drew," Miranda pleaded. "The costumes are for their Halloween party."

Drew sighed and looked up. "Halloween party?" He looked over at Darius. "Is this your doing?"

"Yes, Dad," Darius admitted. "I asked Mom last week. It will be like the last one. Adelaide will be the co-host. We'll do all the cleanup. I promise."

"Fine. But I won't pay for the pizza twice again," Drew said pointedly. He looked back at the paper. "And your sister can't look like"—he gestured—"that. Now finish up. It's almost time to leave for school."

***

Tetsu, Adelaide, Sophie, and Kurt filed off the bus. Rather than continuing to where they usually loitered before the bell, Tetsu stood next to the bus, waiting.

"What are you doing?" Kurt asked confused.

Tetsu crossed his arms and looked at the bus door. "Being a boss."

Adelaide sighed.

Sophie pretended to be disinterested, but stayed close.

Students continued to pour out. Some of them looked at Tetsu warily.

"Just spill it, Julie," Tetsu demanded as Julie stepped off the bus.

"I don't know why you even care," Julie retorted. She looked a little uneasy and glanced nervously between Tetsu and her gaggle of friends waiting for her. It was as if she was trying to calculate if she could make a break for it.

"You've been looking sideways at Kurt the whole bus ride and you were desperate to sit with Sophie even though you ditched her for a week. Just spill it." Tetsu took a step toward her and stood as tall as he could manage.

Adelaide supposed it was mildly imposing.

"Fine," Julie huffed. "It's just that I heard that Parminder—he goes to high school in Olympia—saw Farrah making out with another boy."

She glanced at Kurt, then at Tetsu, and then back

at Kurt again.

"It was on the weekend, but, like I just heard about it last night because that's when, well it doesn't matter who told me. The point is, him and Farrah were in the park and his hands were all over her. Of course, hers were on him, too. They used tongues and everything."

"I'm so sorry, Kurt," Julie said without the slightest remorse. "It must be such terrible news." She flicked her hair over her shoulder and skipped off toward her friends.

Kurt was as still as a statue. All of the colour had drained from his face.

Farrah rounded the corner and smiled when she saw Kurt. "Kurtybear!" she exclaimed.

"Don't 'Kurtybear' me," Kurt retorted in an icy tone that made Adelaide recoil. "I heard what you did! You … you … slut!" Kurt yelled.

Adelaide's chest tightened as he used the slur.

Kids on the playground turned to look.

"Kurt," Adelaide cautioned. What was with her friends lately?

"No!" Kurt yelled. "No! She's a slut!" He pointed at Farrah. "I can call her what she is!"

Farrah's eyes filled with tears and she stumbled backward. "Kurt?" she whispered.

"I heard what you did!" Kurt exclaimed.

Adelaide stood, horrified.

Farrah turned on her heel and ran toward the office.

Sophie's eyes were wide.

"Ooh, yeah, you'll get in trouble for that." Tetsu grimaced.

***

The shiny black Lincoln Town Car pulled into the parking lot outside the school. "Remember," Drew said. "Don't make me wait after school."

"Of course, Daddy," Davia said as she climbed out of the front seat.

"I won't, Dad," Darius promised as he exited the vehicle. He grinned as he caught sight of Adelaide. She hadn't seen him yet. She stood near her bus in a small circle with Kurt, Tetsu, Sophie, and Farrah. As he watched, Farrah spun on her heel and ran for the school doors.

Darius moved away from the car toward Adelaide. He expected his father to back out of his stall and leave the parking lot. Instead, Drew opened the door.

"Adelaide," Drew called.

Darius froze in his tracks.

Adelaide looked over in their direction, her face solemn.

Darius glanced back over at his father who was motioning Adelaide over.

Adelaide looked between Farrah and Drew, and then walked toward the car.

Her eyes caught Darius' as she approached.

"I don't know what it's about," Darius apologized as the two of them made their way back to Drew.

"Adelaide," Drew greeted her. "This party the two of you are hosting. Can your mother supervise? Darius' mother and I are unavailable."

"Oh, I suppose that would be fine. I can ask her. I'll have her call you after school," Adelaide suggested.

"That would be fine. Enjoy the rest of your day." Drew climbed back into his car and closed the door.

"That was it?" Adelaide asked with a frown. She glanced back at the school entrance Farrah had retreated through moments ago.

"Hey, is everything okay? That looked intense," Darius said.

"No." Adelaide sighed. "No, it isn't. I think Kurt's about to get into a lot of trouble. And he sort of deserves it."

Darius searched her face for clues as they walked back toward the others.

"Thanks for the help, Adelaide," Kurt fumed. "She went to the office! Couldn't you have stopped her?"

Adelaide blinked in surprise.

"Kurt," Darius said. "Maybe—"

"Whatever! I don't need this right now," Kurt growled as he stormed off.

"I got it," Sophie said. She gave them a weak smile and ran off after Kurt.

"Can you believe that?" Tetsu asked. "Little Kurt. He sure grew a pair, huh?"

"Tetsu," Adelaide warned.

"Did you want to walk?" Darius asked. He had no idea what was going on, and he was desperate to ask, but he could tell Adelaide wasn't ready to talk about it. "It must be almost time for the bell, but we could talk about the mixed tape," he suggested instead.

Adelaide nodded. She cast one last look back at Tetsu before she fell in step with Darius.

Darius had no idea what had transpired before his arrival, but he desperately hoped it could be resolved before the party on Friday.

Four

The recess bell rang, and the students filed out of Mr. McKenzie's classroom. "Have a great recess!" he called, one tentacle waving. Today he was a mottled red squid.

Adelaide had just exited the building when she saw someone move toward her.

"Hey!" Davia yelled as she stormed over. "Yeah, you." She pointed at Adelaide.

Adelaide looked around confused. "Me?"

"Yes! You! Tell your friend not call people names like that. Got it?"

Davia, who was several inches shorter than Adelaide, tilted her head so she was looking directly at her. Her nose pointed upward and her whole head was angled in such a strange way it was almost comical. Still, she had a fire in her eyes that surprised Adelaide.

Adelaide wanted to say she hated what Kurt had said.

She wanted to tell Kurt he was being a jerk.

She wanted to defend Kurt because she suspected

this might have something to do with everything going on at home.

"I can't control what people do," Adelaide replied instead.

Davia grimaced, grunted in frustration, and stomped her foot before she turned and stalked off.

Adelaide stared after her.

"Ready to talk about this morning?" Darius asked coming up alongside Adelaide.

"Sure," Adelaide sighed.

"You don't have to," Darius insisted.

"It's fine. I guess Farrah cheated on Kurt. He found out. He called her a mean word. To be honest, I'm not impressed with him either. I'm not sure why your sister is mad about it." Adelaide shrugged. "But I don't want to talk to him."

"Then we won't." Darius smiled at her. "So, um, do you want to come over to my house one day this week?"

"In addition to the party?"

"Yes," Darius replied. "Like, you could come over after school and we could just hang out. And you could stay for dinner if you want."

Adelaide thought for a moment. "I don't think I can this week."

Darius tried to hide his disappointment.

"Next week, though. I could come over one day next week." She nodded, either to herself or to him, Darius wasn't sure.

"Yeah?" Darius grinned. "Rad! It's going to be so much fun!"

***

The friends of Pine Street, Tetsu included, had gathered into their usual spots in the basement. The stereo, playing "It's All I Can Do" by The Cars, was the only sound in the basement. Everyone was quiet.

The school day had felt surprisingly long; longer than it ought to have been with the promise of Halloween just around the corner.

Kurt was testy and miserable. Tetsu was his usual self, more or less. Adelaide could tell Sophie's comment about him not being the boss still stung. Darius, who was not present, seemed to be feeling left out lately, but there were some things he couldn't help with. It did not help that he didn't live close enough to pop by after school. Sophie, for her part, was also sullen. And all of it accumulated around Adelaide, swirling in big dark motes that made her feel helpless. She knew if she went home, they would each go home, too, but she didn't think any of them actually wanted to be alone right now and so she sat on the floor, her fingers intertwined in the orange shag carpet, and let the guitar and keyboard music wash over her. There were too many problems, but perhaps she could solve one or two of them.

Kurt's problem was far too big for her. She hoped that being there for him would be enough. She wondered how he had managed not to get called to the office, but she didn't want to bring up the incident.

Darius seemed to be feeling left out, but agreeing to the dinner at his house had brightened his spirits (and she was curious to see what his mother's cooking was like). Adelaide also figured Darius would be happy once they co-hosted the party together. He needed something to do or fix, and the party might be the answer.

Tetsu craved being the centre of attention. She just needed to defer to him once or twice and he would likely feel better, but the opportunity had to present itself.

And then there was Sophie. Sophie did not like this school year. She did not like Davia. She didn't really like Farrah either, even though the two of them *could* be friends. But Sophie wanted it all, so no one else could have it.

There was no way Adelaide could or was even willing to give her everything, but maybe there was something she could offer her friend.

"Sophie?" Adelaide asked.

"What?" Sophie almost barked as she looked up from a well-read issue of *Vogue*.

"How's Amy?"

Sophie's face lightened for a moment, then it clouded over again. "She's fine."

"That's good. Do you get to talk to her much?" Adelaide asked. She could tell the boys were listening intently, though neither looked up.

"Yes," Sophie snapped, defensively. Then she sighed. "No. Her dad won't let us talk. He's decided I'm some sort of bad influence." Sophie's cheeks reddened.

"Really?" Adelaide frowned.

"Yes. It's stupid." Sophie opened her mouth, glanced at the boys, then closed it again. "He's just being stupid."

Adelaide surveyed Sophie's pink cheeks and nodded. Sophie had left something out, but she was not sure what.

"I could call her if you want. Mr. Pecora would

probably let her talk to me, and then I'd just swap the phone over to you," Adelaide offered.

"Really?" Sophie asked. "You'd do that?"

"Why not?" Adelaide shrugged.

"Thanks, Adelaide!" Sophie squealed. She glanced at the wall clock. "She won't be home quite yet, I don't think. Maybe you can call in a bit? You can stay for dinner."

Adelaide glanced at the clock. If she wasn't home for dinner, her mother might not eat, but there was not much in the way of food in the cupboards right now anyway.

"I'll just call my mom and tell her I'm staying late, okay?" Adelaide asked.

"Yeah, sure, whatever. Oh, I can't believe I get to talk to Amy," Sophie twittered.

Tetsu rolled his eyes.

Adelaide smiled. At least there was someone she could help.

***

The air was still as Andy walked Adelaide up the street. It was the perfect evening. Adelaide had stayed at his house for dinner, Sophie had been in a remarkably good mood, and his mother had made shepherd's pie, which was Andy's favourite dish.

Adelaide carried half a dozen records, all borrowed from the collection in Andy's basement.

"Where's your backpack?" Andy asked.

"I took it home earlier," Adelaide explained. "I wanted to check on my mom before dinner."

"Ah. I could carry those, if you want," Andy offered.

"Thank you, but I'm okay," Adelaide said. "It was cool of your parents to let me borrow them for the mixed tape."

"I guess so. They don't mind. Oh, the football team—" Andy grimaced as his voice raised an octave. "They uh, decided to dress up after all."

"What as?" Adelaide asked. She looked over at him.

His heart skipped as beat as her dark eyes met his.

"Hula girls."

"No!" Adelaide gasped. A smile spread across her face. "You'll dress up, too, then?"

Andy flushed and looked away. "I'm thinking about it."

"You should," Adelaide said. Her voice was flat and even, but Andy glanced over and saw a sparkle in her eye.

She paused. "The grass skirts and everything?"

"The grass skirts and everything," Andy confirmed. "It's just …" He closed his eyes. "I can't dance. They want everyone to dance and I can't dance." He opened his eyes and looked over at her. He held his breath and waited for her to laugh.

"Oh." Adelaide pursed her lips and looked deep in thought. "Okay."

They had arrived outside her house now. Andy inhaled deeply and caught the scent of her shampoo. "Well, uh, have a good night."

"Uh-uh. Come in." Adelaide gestured toward the house.

"What?" Andy squeaked.

"You don't have to," Adelaide said.

"No, I, uh, okay," Andy said as he glanced around. "Okay."

They walked up the front steps and then Adelaide tried to juggle the records with one hand while she fished the key out of her pocket with the other.

"Here, please," Andy said as he took the records.

"Thank you," she said with a little smile. "It would be terrible if I dropped them."

Andy nodded, still stunned he was going to get to

spend more time with Adelaide. In her house, no less.

Adelaide put the key in the lock, turned it, then opened the door. She stepped inside and indicated he should follow.

"Where, um, where do you want these?" Andy asked as he used the heel of one shoe to remove the other.

"Oh, here, let me take them," Adelaide said as she put her own shoes in the front closet.

Their fingers touched as she took the records back. Andy blushed. He hoped Adelaide didn't notice.

"In here," Adelaide said as she walked through a doorway into the adjacent living room. She moved over to the stereo, set the stack of records down, and rifled through her own collection.

Andy glanced around the room. The furniture was worn, but the room itself was beautiful. It had high ceilings and where the walls and ceiling met was fancy. Andy thought it was called crown molding. The wooden floors were dented and worn, but as he looked around, it was as though he could see something just below the surface. It was as if the whole house was sitting quietly, waiting for someone to pay attention to it.

"This is it," Adelaide murmured as she pulled a large black disc out of a record case. She set it on the turn table and moved the record needle.

She sighed contentedly and closed her eyes.

Andy watched as she smiled at the hiss that emanated from the speakers before the first sounds of recorded music played.

It was the Beach Boys. "Surfin' USA."

Adelaide opened her eyes and stepped toward to Andy.

"So, you just …" Adelaide swayed her hips side to side, her arms stretched out to the right, gently waving them up and down.

Andy stared, mesmerised.

"Come on, you try," she encouraged.

She was closer now.

"Uh …" Andy tried to move. He felt awkward.

She smiled over at him. "A little more of this." Her hips swayed back and forth.

"I don't …"

"Just like this," Adelaide said as she reached over and placed her hands on either side of his waist.

Andy tried to move how she indicated, but he tripped on his foot as he shuffled. He tried to regain his footing, but he pitched forward and landed on top of Adelaide, against the couch.

"I am so sorry," Andy squeaked, mortified.

He grimaced as he clambered to his feet. He could feel flames on his cheeks and was sure they were bright red. "I should go. I have to go. I'm so sorry." Andy held onto Adelaide's arm and helped her get back to her feet. Then he put his head down and ran for the door.

Five

The rain was light this morning, but the sky was dark and ominous. Gus Zillman had been in a worse mood than usual, which put Agatha Zillman in an equally worse mood. Without discussing it, Adelaide and Tetsu had started waiting in front of Sophie's house for Kurt. Adelaide scanned the front window of the Zillman house as Kurt descended the steps. Mrs. Zillman stood, scowling out the window at Adelaide through narrowed eyes. Her lips were pursed, and her arms were folded.

Adelaide met her gaze, then turned away as the Katillion's front door opened and Sophie walked down the front steps. Her backpack hung off her shoulder, but she carried a lunch bag in her hands, which she handed to Adelaide without a word.

"You won't put up with this, right?" Tetsu demanded of Kurt.

"What?" Kurt asked confused. The skin around his eye had lightened to a sickly brownish yellow, but it was still a nasty shiner.

"Some guy kissed your girl. You have to show them both who's boss," Tetsu explained.

"What?" Kurt asked again.

"Look, here's the plan. We take that rod of Kyber's, then we go over—"

"Whatever you are about to say, the answer is no," Kurt cut in. "It's done. I don't want some slut for a girlfriend anyway."

Adelaide felt her insides boiling over. "Both of you stop it!" she exclaimed, the words rising up and out of her before she could stop them.

Everyone's steps faltered.

Adelaide kept walking, but the roiling anger inside her hadn't subsided.

"Both of you are acting like such *jerks*," she called over her shoulder.

It was unusual for her to raise her voice, but she couldn't help it. She stalked to the bus stop at the end of the road and by the time she arrived, she felt as though she could breathe again.

The others arrived a few moments later.

Tetsu and Kurt looked sheepish.

Sophie, Adelaide thought, seemed mildly impressed.

Adelaide glowered down the road in the direction the bus would arrive from.

They all stood in silence. Even the other kids at the stop sensed something was amiss and decided to hold their tongues.

The two front benches of the school bus were quiet the whole trip to the school. It felt like the longest bus ride of the year so far, and Adelaide wished she had music to listen to. She had seen some people with Walkmans, and while she would have loved one, she preferred to eat.

As they stepped off the bus, Kurt fell in alongside Adelaide.

"Adelaide, I have to talk to you," Kurt said. "Privately."

"What is it, Kurt?" Adelaide asked. "Unless it's an apology, I'm not in the mood."

"It's important," Kurt insisted. "And I *am* sorry if I upset you."

Adelaide pursed her lips and appraised Kurt. It was a weak apology, but it was more sincere than one of Tetsu's half-hearted attempts. And Kurt looked worried.

"Fine," she relented and the two of them walked toward the field, and away from the building itself. "If you're worried Tetsu will get his hands on the rod, don't be. I've hidden it. It's too dangerous for any of us to play with."

"No, it's not that," Kurt said.

They continued walking. When they were out of earshot, Kurt leaned in. "I don't really know how to say this, it's just … my mom has been talking a lot about making a phone call."

Adelaide looked at him expectantly. "Okay …"

"It's to her friend, Nancy. Nancy works for … she works for Child Protective Services."

Adelaide's steps wavered. She felt a weird tingling sensation on her skin. "Why do I need to know that, Kurt?"

Kurt's eyes looked sad. "You know why. She doesn't think your mom …"

"What did you say? Did she make the call? Is her friend … going to pay a visit?" Adelaide asked as lightly as she could. The tingling was not stopping and her face felt strangely warm. Everything looked different, too, like she could not quite see clearly.

"I said you were fine, that your mom was fine. But then my dad got mad about something. I couldn't push anything after that, not unless—" Kurt gestured to his face. "I thought I was getting somewhere, Adelaide. I did. But then with my dad … she might have forgotten what I said. But maybe she won't call. I'm really sorry. I just thought you should know. It sounded like Nancy would be doing her a favour, like it wasn't exactly official, so maybe nothing will happen." Kurt was close to tears. "Maybe she won't even call."

"You did what you could," Adelaide assured him. "Thanks for the warning."

"I'm really sorry."

"You don't have any reason to be," Adelaide said. "I'll figure it out. I'll see you in class, okay?"

Before Kurt could answer, Adelaide doubled back across the field. The irony of Kurt's mother calling Child Protective Services was not lost on Adelaide. She wondered if Mrs. Zillman was trying to deflect any unwanted attention from her own family by directing them elsewhere. A trick of misdirection. Emotions coursed through her like waves slamming into the shore.

She needed to be alone.

***

Drew Belcouer pulled up outside of James Morrison Elementary School.

"And remember, don't be late," Drew instructed.

"I won't, Dad," Darius said. He shouldered his backpack and climbed out of the backseat of the car.

"Of course, Daddy," Davia said. She emerged from the front seat and flicked her blond hair over her shoulder as she did so.

Darius wondered if she had her fingers crossed behind her back. He could not recall a single time he had been late to meet his father, that was under his control anyway. His sister, Davia, on the other hand was another story.

"Behave," Drew said as they closed their doors.

Darius nodded, but his father was already gone, racing through the parking lot toward the exit. He looked around and spotted Kurt and Tetsu in their usual spot, but Adelaide wasn't with them.

"Hey guys," he said as he approached. "Where's Adelaide?"

"She, um … she wanted some space," Kurt said.

"What happened?" Darius asked. He looked back and forth across the schoolyard. Had she been hurt? Had he said something to offend her? He turned to Tetsu and narrowed his eyes. "What did you say?"

"Me?" Tetsu balked. "I didn't say nothin'."

151

"That's true," Kurt reminded him. "She was mad at both of us."

"For what?" Darius asked. "Where is she?"

Kurt opened his mouth as if he was going to say something, then closed it again. He took a deep breath. "She's over in the field, but it'd be best to just wait. Adelaide sort of … she'll talk when she's ready."

"Or she won't," Tetsu said. "I know. I'm her best friend."

Darius concentrated on his breath and gently shook his hands. Sometimes he hated Tetsu.

***

When the bell rang, Adelaide walked slowly to class. Only the last few stragglers were still in the cloakroom and she hung up her raincoat and backpack with little more than a nod of a greeting.

She could feel her friends' eyes on her, but she kept her gaze down and slipped into her usual seat just as Mr. McKenzie, dressed in a puffy black and yellow bee costume, began taking attendance.

Six

Darius smoothed his linen napkin on his lap and looked around the long wooden table. An array of dishes had been neatly arranged down the centre.

"This smells really good," he said.

"It should, for what we pay," Drew grumbled.

"Not this again, dear, please," Miranda pleaded.

"Fine. Pass the gravy," Drew replied.

"Darius, dear," Miranda cooed, as she passed the gravy boat to her husband, "how is everything at school?"

"It's fine, Mom," Darius said. "Thanks for asking."

He tried to poke his fork into a piece of roasted potato, but the potato slipped out of the way. He adjusted, and jabbed a bit harder.

"And you're okay? I mean you aren't getting"—she glanced at his plate—"frustrated?"

Darius forced himself not to grimace. He had really hoped they were past this. There had not been a single incident since they had moved from Boston. People like Tetsu bugged him sometimes, sure, but he had kept his temper. He liked Olympic Vista.

"It's okay to feel frustrated. Even angry," Miranda said.

"I'm not angry, Mom." Darius' voice was even and calm, but he was starting to become irritated. He could not understand why his mother didn't realize that if you looked for a problem, you would find one. Or make one.

"Darius, I'm not sure I like your tone," Miranda warned.

"You have to be kidding me!" Darius exclaimed. "What's wrong with my tone?"

"Darius," Drew warned. "Don't speak to your mother like that. We won't put up with another incident. I *will* send you to boarding school."

Darius looked around confused.

Davia smirked over the rim of her glass.

"Of course," Darius said, lowering his voice. He forced a smile across his face. "I apologize."

Davia stabbed her fork into a potato.

Their parents did not seem to notice.

Darius took great pains to gently nudge another potato onto his fork with his knife. He wondered how his parents would feel if someone repeatedly asked them if they were all right.

***

Adelaide climbed off her bike and leaned it against the back wall of the house. She pulled two paper bags out of the rear basket and carried them around the house. The money Tetsu had slipped Adelaide earlier in the week had allowed her to pick up a few things from Rutledge's, the local corner store. She juggled the bags in one hand to close the side gate, then proceeded up the front steps where she let herself in and locked the door behind her.

The house was quiet.

Adelaide set the bags down, shrugged off her wet coat and slipped off her shoes. She put them away in the closet, and then carried the bags into the kitchen. She had meant to go shopping yesterday, but then Mrs. Katillion had invited her to stay for dinner. Adelaide knew her house needed some groceries anyway, but if there was any chance someone official might check up on her … Adelaide shuddered at the thought of it.

Adelaide pulled a can of tomato soup from one of the bags, opened it, and dumped the contents into a pot.

It landed with a splat. Most of it was still shaped like a cylinder; little ringed indentations rising the height of the red glob.

Adelaide filled the can with water and added it to the pot.

Gelatinous blobs of soup floated in the puddle of water.

Adelaide glanced toward the front hall where the stairs led to the second floor. She was not sure if Violet was home, but no one else seemed to be. She glanced at the clock. It was after six o'clock and she was hungry.

Adelaide considered her options. She could eat a sandwich, but she wanted something hot. The adults in the house did not like her using the stove without supervision. However, she was fairly certain she was as responsible as at least half of them.

Adelaide turned the element on low and gave the pot contents a quick stir before she unpacked the rest of the groceries. She put several pieces of fruit into a glass bowl on the table, and an apple straight into her lunch kit. Then she slid two boxes of cereal and some peanut butter into the cupboard and put two loaves of bread into the breadbox.

She stirred the soup, but it was not quite warm enough.

Adelaide wiped the counter, which was covered with crumbs and dried droplets of coffee, and pulled the broom from the cupboard. She swept up dirt and debris on the floor and tipped it all from the dustpan into the garbage can.

She tried the soup again. She nodded to herself, turned off the element, and served it up in a bowl.

The rest of the cleaning could wait until she had eaten.

Seven

Wednesday turned into Thursday, which was largely uneventful. By now, pumpkins on front porches were carved into jack-o'-lanterns. The weather was chillier. Mr. McKenzie continued to entertain the students with his array of costumes. Today he was a narwhal. And students at the school could not stop buzzing about the coming holiday, their costumes (many of which were from the amazing new costume shop), and all the candy they hoped to devour.

Some classmates were hesitant to forgo trick-or-treating for a Halloween party, but Darius' promise of pizza and bowls of treats won over most of the seventh grade.

Kurt had painstakingly collected everything he needed to dress up as his idol, Albert Einstein. Sophie was still thrilled her mother had purchased a brand-new costume for her this year (rather than her usual cobbled-together-homemade-costume). Tetsu couldn't stop talking about his authentic ninja garb. And Darius had grinned all week at the idea of matching costumes with Adelaide, who had decided to wear her mother's old cheerleading uniform.

The most exciting thing about Thursday had been when Belinda arrived home with the ingredients for popcorn balls. She had insisted that Adelaide, as co-host of the party, should bring something to contribute. Belinda had dusted off an old family recipe book that Adelaide had never seen her use before. Thanks to Adelaide's efforts, none of the ingredients had burned. The popcorn balls came out nearly perfect, and Belinda beamed proudly for the rest of the week.

Most of the kids at the school behaved as though they were already amped up on sugar. Belinda, who was thrilled to be chaperoning the party, was not any better. Adelaide was convinced her mother had replaced their Halloween candy twice this week, having consumed the first two bags when left to her own devices after Adelaide had gone to bed. Adelaide had no idea where her mother had gotten the money for the candy or popcorn ball ingredients (or why she had not used that money for groceries), but she consoled herself with the fact that she had been able to add a mini-Mars Bar to her lunch.

And then, suddenly, it was Friday.

The friends of Pine Street climbed off the bus outside James Morrison Elementary. Tetsu was dressed as a ninja, Sophie as a witch (with a convincing fake hooked nose and long grey hair), and Kurt had a homemade Albert Einstein costume. For her part, Adelaide wore her mother's old cheerleading uniform over a long-sleeved white top and a pair of thick tights. She knew it was not exactly authentic, but she was not overly interested in sporting a short skirt and short sleeves in the fall.

Brody, who had allegedly doodled hearts around his and Adelaide's initials in his notebook last year, walked up to Adelaide. He was wearing a suit and carried a plush dog under one arm. A single boot dangled from his backpack.

"I like your costume, Adelaide. It suits you." He smiled at her. "Will you wear it to the party tonight?"

"That's my plan. And thank you. It was my mom's."

"Rad! Do you know who I am?" he asked hopefully.

Adelaide studied him for moment.

"The Monopoly Man," she guessed.

He grinned. "You got it. I made it myself!"

"You did a nice job," Adelaide said. She was surprised Brody's costume wasn't video game related considering how often he rattled on about his Nintendo.

"Yeah?" Brody looked relieved. He rubbed his neck

with fat sausage fingers. "So many kids this year got their costume from that weird emporium. It's hard to compete with that."

"I don't think we have to. Halloween should be about having fun."

"Yeah! I guess it should be. Plus, Arthur said the guy selling the costumes is super creepy." Brody shuddered. "I'm all about the candy, not the creepy."

"Candy is good," Adelaide said, uncertain how else to respond. She wanted to be kind, but she didn't want to encourage him too much, not after everyone had teased her about the crush he had on her. Adelaide was about to ask what else Arthur had said about the man at the costume shop when Darius ran up to them. He wore an authentic-looking football uniform.

"You look perfect!" Darius proclaimed as he took in Adelaide's cheer uniform. "Nice costume, Brody. Rich Uncle Pennybags, right? From Monopoly."

"Yep, thanks, Darius."

Darius turned back to Adelaide. "Check it! What do you think?" He grinned at Adelaide as he gestured at his uniform.

Adelaide smiled. "It looks good."

"Right? Cheer captain and football quarterback.

Perfect together. So, do you want to go steady?" Darius grinned.

"We do look good together," Adelaide agreed. She couldn't tell if Darius had made a joke, or if he was being serious. She couldn't help smile back at Darius' grin. Adelaide loved the way he wore his heart on his sleeve.

She thought of Kurt's reaction to Farrah's infidelity and to the number of men her own mother had allowed through the house. Most of all, she thought of dancing with Andy in her living room.

Adelaide picked at the cuticle of her index finger with her thumb. She felt pulled in too many directions.

The bell rang, and Adelaide put Darius' question out of her mind.

***

Darius took his seat at his desk, ran his fingers through his hair and looked around.

Everyone wore some sort of costume. Wiltshire Preparatory Academy had a strict uniform policy, even on Halloween. He grinned. Everything about Olympic Vista was better than Boston.

Adelaide's solemn face stared up at the front of the

classroom where Mr. McKenzie had begun to take his morning attendance while dressed as a genuine French chef.

Her costume was everything Darius had hoped it would be. He could picture her a couple of years from now, cheerleading at the high school in an ironic sort of way. He did not see himself as a football player. Team sports didn't appeal to him. But he would dress up as one every year for the rest of his life if it meant matching costumes with Adelaide.

She had thought he had been joking this morning, but he hadn't been.

"Darius," Adelaide said. She nudged his foot with her own.

"What?"

She nodded toward the front of the class.

"Daydreaming I see, Darius," Mr. McKenzie said with a chuckle.

"Oh, sorry, um, here," Darius stammered.

There was a small chorus of laughter around the classroom (Darius was convinced Tetsu was the loudest), but Mr. McKenzie brought everyone to attention and continued with the attendance.

Darius had thought the day would pass slowly.

Instead, Mr. McKenzie, who never ceased to surprise Darius, made the day fun by dividing the class into teams and holding a competition to see which team could answer the most questions correctly. Darius and Adelaide were on the same side, but they were no match for Kurt's team.

Kurt was like a walking encyclopedia, answering more questions than anyone else, and always with the correct answer. After the final question had been read, and Kurt had dinged the little bell and answered correctly, Mr. McKenzie handed out candy. The winning side got theirs first, but the prize was the same for both sides.

The desks were moved back to their usual positions and everyone took their seats.

"Ha, you won and we got the same thing," Tetsu said. He unwrapped his candy and shoved it into his mouth.

"That's *so* not fair," Sophie pouted quietly when everyone resumed their usual seats.

"We almost got the same thing. Sophie and I, and the rest of our team, received the satisfaction of winning," Kurt replied.

Darius stifled a laugh.

"He's got a point," Adelaide said to Tetsu. "They

have bragging rights."

"Whatever," Tetsu said, as he slurped on his candy. "Are you going to eat yours?"

Adelaide shrugged and handed it over.

"Do you want mine?" Darius asked Adelaide.

Tetsu smirked. "Sure, I'll take it."

"Not you," Darius said. "Adelaide?"

"Oh, thanks, Darius. That's nice of you." Adelaide took the candy from Darius and tucked it into her pocket. "I'm looking forward to the party tonight. And it'll be fun to come over after school."

"Yeah, it's going to be rad," Darius said. He ran his fingers through his hair again. "We'll get time, just us, before the party." He could hardly wait.

"Wait, what?" Tetsu asked, slurping his candy. "Won't your sister be there or something?"

"Maybe. I think she'll be too busy getting ready, though," Darius said, and he hoped it was true.

Tetsu scowled, but Darius ignored him and grinned.

Eight

Drew Belcouer pulled his shiny black car into his driveway and shifted it into park. He did not cut the engine. Darius scrambled out of the car and held the door open for Adelaide. Davia climbed out of the front seat and Darius could feel her eyes roll at his attempt of chivalry.

Adelaide climbed out of the backseat.

"Thank you for the ride, Mr. Belcouer," she said.

"You're welcome," Drew replied. "If you'll excuse me, I have to get back to the office. Your mother will be here soon, yes?"

"She should be, yes."

"Very good." Drew put the car into reverse and looked at Darius expectantly.

"Thanks, Dad," Darius said as closed the door.

Drew turned the car around in the driveway and retreated toward the road without another word. Darius saw the front door close and guessed Davia had already gone in.

"Is he always like that?" Adelaide asked.

"Pretty much." Darius led Adelaide around the house into the backyard.

Adelaide followed him quietly as he opened the pool house door and led her inside. There were already bags of chips set out, two-litre bottles of soda and trays of snacks in the fridge, and decorations piled up on the counter waiting to be tacked on the walls.

"I meant it, you know," Darius said in as light a tone as he could manage. He wiped his sweaty palms on the polyester pants of his costume.

"Meant what?" Adelaide asked as she picked up two rolls of crêpe paper, one black and one orange.

Her voice was devoid of tone and Darius wished he could read her mind.

"About going steady. I meant it."

There. It was out there now.

"Oh. Well, I mean … I suppose we could try it. But what if … I like our friendship, Darius."

"Friends forever, either way." Darius grinned at her nervously. "I promise. No matter what." Darius lifted his hand toward his mouth and spat on it. He extended it out to Adelaide. "We'll shake on it."

A smile spread across Adelaide's face. "You mean to

tell me, we'll shake hands with spit on them, and even if we break up, you'll always be my friend no matter what? You won't act in that stupid way people do when they get their heart broken?"

"I promise." Darius lifted his spit covered hand toward his chest and used a finger to draw a cross over his heart. "Cross my heart." He extended his hand, which still had a gob of spit in the palm, back out to Adelaide.

She paused for just a moment before she spat on her own hand and clasped it to his.

"Deal, then." There was still a smile on her face.

Darius promised himself he would make her smile like that as often as he could.

***

Andy sat up and tugged at the bottom of his sport coat with his free hand. He had hoped to find an actual suit, but the dress pants and sport coat worked well enough. He had taken great care ironing his own shirt. It was the plastic water gun on the couch next to him that completed the ensemble. He had even taken the time to paint it black.

"Sophie, dear! It's time to go," Sheila called.

Andy looked up from his copy of *On Her Majesty's Secret Service.*

"Time for you to go?" Andy asked.

"Yes, sweetie. We'll drop Sophie and her friends at the party, then we're off to our party. You've got the number, right?" Sheila adjusted the devil horns she had placed on her head. She wore a form fitting red dress and she wore red tights over her legs and arms. "Oh! Here, I cut you up some apple." She set a plate of apple slices on the coffee table.

"Thanks, Mom," Andy said. "Your costume looks good. Very authentic. Got a pitch fork?"

"Thank you! And yes, it's by the door. Where is your father?"

Andy picked up a slice of apple and took a bite.

"And you're sure you're okay with this, champ?" Jack asked, as if on cue, as he waddled into the room. He wore a long green cylinder on his body and a green cone on his head.

"I'm fine, Dad," Andy assured him. "And you are one authentic crayon. Isn't that something?"

"We don't have to go if you aren't comfortable staying home alone," Jack said.

"Dad?" Andy asked.

"Yes, son?" Jack adjusted the cone on his head that represented the tip of the crayon.

"I won't eat the candy. I know you count every piece and calculate your Halloween expenditures perfectly. I won't eat it," Andy promised him.

Jack breathed an audible sigh of relief. "Okay, then. You'll do great. We'll be home later."

Andy nodded. "I'll be fine."

There was a knock at the door.

"Sheila!" Jack called. "It's time to go."

"I know that, dear. I'm right here," Sheila shook her head. She kissed Andy's hair. "She went to the party early," she whispered.

"Who? What?" Andy squeaked. Disappointment flooded through his body. He had heard from Sophie that Adelaide had dressed up as a cheerleader for Halloween. He had hoped to see her in her costume, but more than that, he had just wanted to see her.

Sheila smiled and gave him a wave as she headed for the front door.

Tetsu and Kurt burst through the door and Sophie emerged from her room to greet them. Everyone fussed with shoes on the landing and Andy tried not to laugh when his dad got stuck on the steps and could not stand up without help.

Within a few minutes, the house was quiet.

Andy looked around, pulled the black water pistol from his pocket, and skirted the edge of the hallway. He raised the gun in front of him and swivelled to face inside his bedroom.

He swept the gun across the room as he scanned it.

He raised one hand to his ear.

"All clear," he said. He moved in front of the mirror and took in his reflection.

"Katillion. Andy Katillion," he said as he raised his eyebrows.

"Katillion. Andy Katillion," he said again with a half smile.

He shook his head at himself.

Then he sighed and flopped on the bed.

***

Most of the seventh-grade students milled around the pool deck or congregated inside the pool house. Belinda, who was dressed as a black cat, kept to the fringes of the party and greeted parents as they dropped off their children. Almost everyone was here now, and

Belinda tried to remain inconspicuous.

Adelaide smiled at her, then looked around. She did not see her herself as an overly popular person, and yet every person here had greeted her warmly. They seemed happy to see her. It was a strange thing that had been happening lately, and she didn't dislike it. It just took some getting used to.

The party was a huge success, perhaps even more so than their previous party, and yet something nagged at Adelaide.

Sophie leaned against the outside wall of the pool house chatting with Ashley, who was dressed as a ballerina, and Farrah, who was dressed up as a fox. Farrah was studiously ignoring Kurt, who had been cornered by Nelson nearby. Nelson seemed to be giving Kurt the third degree about something, and Kurt, for his part, looked disinterested.

Colin and Reggie wandered out from behind a tree sniggering. Colin wore a red and black striped shirt and black pants, and Reggie was in all black with an oversized coat and carried a cheap white plastic hockey mask. Colin pulled on a rubber head mask, complete with a black hat.

"The fridge is full of big bottles of soda," Tetsu exclaimed as he walked up to Adelaide, a red cup in each hand. "And it's all name brand. Not any of that generic knock-off shit."

"It was last time, too," Adelaide said.

"I know, but it's rad. I wish I lived here."

"If you lived here, Tetsu, you'd live here with your parents and the fridge would be stocked with the same things it is at home." Adelaide looked at him pointedly. "Is one of those for me?"

"Why you gotta ruin my fun?" Tetsu asked. He took a big gulp from one of the cups, then smacked his lips in satisfaction. "And, uh …" He glanced longingly at the second cup. "Yeah, this is for you."

Adelaide accepted the cup and took a big sip. It was cold and fizzy.

"Pizza's here!" someone yelled.

"Pizza!" a chorus of voices responded.

Adelaide glanced over. A trail of people followed Darius, who was carrying a stack of pizza boxes, into the pool house.

"Come on," Adelaide said. "We'll even refill that cup for you."

"There's the friend I know and love," Tetsu said. "Or, you know what I mean …"

Adelaide shook her head. He had been acting

strangely lately.

She led them through the throng of classmates toward the boxes.

"Eww. What's on that one?" Davia, wearing a Princess Leia costume, asked. Even at a glance, the dress was obviously of the highest quality. The light glinted off the ray gun tucked into Davia's belt, and Adelaide admired whatever finish had been used. It did not look like a toy.

"Spicy peppers. It's Adelaide's," Darius said. He put two slices of the pizza on a paper plate and pushed his way to Adelaide. "For you." He held out the plate.

"Thanks, Darius," Adelaide said. She still was not sure how she felt about having a boyfriend, but so far it was nice. She forced herself not to think about Andy.

"Did you grab me some?" Tetsu asked with a scowl.

"It's right there," Darius said. He pointed at the boxes just a few feet away.

"Fine, whatever." Tetsu turned and pushed through a group of people as he navigated his way to the pizza boxes.

"Are you going to get a slice?" Adelaide asked Darius.

Arthur, dressed in a convincing werewolf costume,

tried to step out of Tetsu's way, but he startled Heather, who spilled soda on her Strawberry Shortcake costume.

"Sorry, Heather," Arthur squeaked in the most un-wolflike fashion.

"Ack!" Heather's eyes welled up with tears. "I hope this comes out," she said as she ran for the bathroom.

"I'm good right now. Did you want to—" Darius gestured toward a corner of the room where a few seats had become available.

Adelaide nodded and they moved through the room to the sound of Joe Jackson singing "Is She Really Going Out with Him?"

"There's pizza, Brody," Adelaide said as they passed the Frogger arcade cabinet.

"Thanks!" Brody called. "I'm good." He jerked the joystick, navigating his frog avatar out of the way of a truck, onto the riverbank, and then onto a log. He was in the same costume as earlier, and his plush dog sat on the floor, propped up against the cabinet.

"I think the party is a hit. We pulled it off, again," Darius said. He was grinning at her, the way he did so often.

Adelaide glanced up and noticed a few party goers being jostled as someone pushed their way forward. More people desperate for a slice of pizza, Adelaide suspected.

"Be careful. You'll jinx it," she said.

"I don't think that's how it—"

"Adelaide!" Kurt called as he shoved his way through the crowd. "Adelaide! Sophie won't wake up."

Nine

Kurt was frantic. He grabbed Adelaide's arm and pulled her toward the door. "We have to help Sophie," Kurt urged.

"What do you mean?" Adelaide asked. "What happened?"

Kurt led her outside to a pool chair.

Sophie was passed out in her witch's costume.

Adelaide walked over, grasped Sophie's shoulders and shook them. "Sophie? Sophie, come on," Adelaide coaxed.

"I tried that," Kurt fretted.

"What did she eat? Or drink?" Adelaide looked around the pool deck and back through the open door to the party. A few other kids looked woozy.

"It hurts," Julie moaned from the pool house.

"Keep an eye on her, okay?" Adelaide said to Kurt as she hurried back to the pool house.

"It hurts," Julie called again. She clutched her stomach, bent over double.

Marcie and Jenny, who were dressed as the Queen of Hearts and one of her minions, had collapsed on the ground.

"Darius?" Adelaide called. She scanned the room and saw him.

Darius, in his football costume with its big shoulder pads and numbered jersey, looked over at her and grinned. The grin turned to a yawn, and he collapsed to the floor.

All around her, Adelaide's classmates were crumpling to the ground.

Tetsu lay in a heap near the counter in the kitchen. There was a piece of pizza and a plastic cup on the floor next to him.

"Kurt!" Adelaide called from the doorway. "There's more in here."

Kurt ran in from the pool deck.

"Oh geez … what do we do?" Kurt gaped.

"I …" Adelaide surveyed the room.

Not everyone had collapsed.

Belinda, likely drawn by calls for Kurt, stepped in from outside. Her eyes were wide with panic.

Julie still clutched her stomach and moaned in pain. The mane of her unicorn costume shimmered and her bodysuit looked softer than ever.

Brody jerked the joystick on the Frogger cabinet, unaware of the chaos around him.

"What's going on?" Ashley squealed. The look of horror on her face was a stark contrast to her pink leotard and tutu. Adelaide recalled Ashley's older sister had attended ballet lessons for a while.

Adelaide looked at Kurt in his old Einstein wig, then down at her own homemade costume.

"It's the costumes, Kurt. The ones from that store. Help me get Tetsu out of his. Maybe he'll wake up."

Kurt bent down and the two of them started to pull Tetsu's ninja-yoroi off.

Tetsu's eyes snapped open. He leapt to his feet and drew the ninjatō from his waist. The light glinted off the blade. Tetsu's eyes were wild as he scanned the room.

"That looks sharp," Kurt said.

Adelaide nodded in agreement. She held her hand up in front of her, trying to signal she didn't pose a threat to him. "Tetsu! It's me, Adelaide," she coaxed.

Tetsu spoke sharply, and quickly, in Japanese.

Adelaide couldn't understand any of it.

"Adelaide? Baby?" Belinda called. "What is this?"

Julie's moans turned to a shriek. There was a

wrenching sound and Adelaide looked over to see a white unicorn where Julie had been a moment ago.

"When do I turn into Jason?" Reggie sniggered.

Colin looked around stupidly.

From the pool deck, someone cackled.

"Off with their heads!" Marcie shrieked as she and Jenny stood up.

Julie-the-Unicorn pranced about the living room, bumping into the table and knocking over some cups.

Tetsu crouched into a defensive stance and held his blade at the ready.

"They are all—oh crap. What about …" Adelaide started as she recalled Arthur's costume.

"Adelaide?" Belinda called weakly.

Kurt's eyes, which were already wide, turned to saucers as a growl sounded from the next room.

A furry, fanged monstrosity slunk through the doorway.

Kurt gasped. "I've got a bad feeling about this."

Ten

Several small blasts of blue light shot across the room and punched the werewolf in the chest.

Adelaide reeled and saw Princess Leia brandishing her blaster.

"He was one of Vader's minions and a threat to the rebellion," Davia declared. "Are you?"

"No," Adelaide said shaking her head. "I'm sure I'm not. Is he dead?" Adelaide ran forward. She could not find a pulse, but she could see the werewolf's chest rise and fall.

"Who do you take me for? Some nerfhearder?" Davia asked in an unfamiliar tone. "I set it to stun."

"What is happening?" Brody cried from the arcade machine.

"Have you seen Obi-wan Kenobi?" Davia asked. "He's my only hope."

"Of course, he is," Adelaide said as she looked up at Davia. "Thanks for your help."

Brody cowered next to the machine.

Kurt did not seem to know where to look or what to do. Adelaide had never seen a deer in headlights, but seeing Kurt frozen to the spot, she had a good idea of what it would look like.

Tetsu spoke quickly again, but Adelaide still could not make out any of it. He stood poised to attack.

She pursed her lips and stood. "Can I just ..." Adelaide reached out and took the blaster from Davia's hands.

"You can't—"

"I'm sorry," Adelaide said. She aimed the blaster at Tetsu and fired.

Tetsu collapsed to the ground.

Adelaide turned to Jenny and Marcie who had moved toward Brody.

"Off with his head!" Marcie screamed at Jenny.

Brody pressed himself against the cabinet and whimpered.

Adelaide aimed and fired at Jenny, who also collapsed. She turned, shifted the blaster to line up another shot, and pulled the trigger.

Marcie collapsed.

Brody gaped.

"This is great," Adelaide said assessing the blaster.

"Check on Sophie," she directed Kurt.

He nodded and stumbled toward the exit.

Adelaide scanned the room and decided a unicorn prancing over the furniture was a potential hazard. She fired at Julie the unicorn and she collapsed to the ground, too.

"Are you sure you are part of the Rebel Alliance?" Davia asked.

"Of course," Adelaide lied. "You're in danger here. Obi-wan is your only hope."

Princess Leia nodded. "All right. I trust you."

Darius ran over in his football uniform.

"Are you okay?" he asked Adelaide, his eyes full of concern.

"I'm okay. Are you okay?" Adelaide asked. She eyed him warily.

"Of course, I am. I can't believe all this. We might miss the big game," Darius exclaimed. "And I have to be there. I'm going to win it for you, babe. You'll see how much I care about you. And when your parents meet me, they'll see I have the best of intentions."

"Darius?" Adelaide asked.

"I love you, Jessica. I've always loved you. I've loved you since that first day we met in kindergarten."

They had not met in kindergarten. They had not met until about two months ago. And her name was not Jessica.

Adelaide sighed. "Darius, I'm sorry." She turned the blaster on him and fired.

He collapsed to the ground. She had only had a boyfriend for a few hours and she had already shot him.

There was a cackle and Adelaide turned toward the door where Sophie stood with Kurt. Several kids in homemade costumes pushed past them to flee to the pool deck.

"What have we here?" Sophie grated in an unfamiliar voice.

"Kurt?" Adelaide asked as she levelled the blaster at Sophie.

"She seems harmless." Kurt shrugged.

"Baby?" Belinda asked, as she cowered in the corner.

"Mama." Adelaide walked over.

"This isn't what I signed up for," Belinda whispered as she looked around.

"I know, Mama. I'm sorry. Can you just, um, keep an eye on everyone?" Adelaide asked.

"Your party is not as you wished it, my dear," Sophie the witch declared. "Perhaps you'd like it to be different?"

"I just need everyone to stop," Adelaide said as she looked around. "Someone could get hurt."

Sophie flexed her fingers and then began to wiggle them. "The trouble here is far too deep, it's time now for most of you to sleep."

People all around the room crumpled to the ground. Sophie the witch, Kurt, Davia (who seemed convinced she was Princess Leia) and Adelaide remained on their feet.

"The Force is strong with you, witch," Davia said.

"Okay, that's good. Good work, Sophie. Can I call you Sophie?" Adelaide asked.

"I am Magrathea the Magnificent, the most powerful witch in all the world," Sophie announced with a cackle.

"All right then." Adelaide turned to Kurt. "I don't think we should leave them like this, but we have to go to the costume store."

"We could call the police," Kurt suggested, hopefully.

Adelaide frowned. "Maybe. Do you think they'll believe us? And if they do, it will take too long." Adelaide walked to the door and looked outside. The rest of the guests had collapsed out there. She walked over to her mother and arranged her in what looked like a slightly more comfortable position for a nap.

"It's not anywhere near here, Adelaide," Kurt said.

"I know, Kurt. What choice do we have?" Adelaide asked. She looked over and saw Darius start to stir. She held her breath and hoped he had shaken off whatever this was.

"Jessica, my love. You're okay," he said as he looked at Adelaide. "Whatever this witch has done, it can't stop my love for you."

"Oh, wow," Kurt murmured.

"We have to play along," Adelaide hissed at Kurt. "Ask him his name."

"Uh, who are you?" Kurt asked.

"I'm Dick. The best quarterback the team has ever seen," Darius said, standing up. He looked at Adelaide and rolled his eyes, incredulous someone could ask such a question.

"Sorry, Dick. He isn't from around here," Adelaide lied. "And this isn't Magrathea's fault. She wants to help. I think." Adelaide glanced at Sophie and back at Darius. "Can you help us, or not? We have to, uh, defeat the foul magic that is a threat to the Rebellion."

"For you? I can do it. My love for you will see us

through," Darius declared.

"Wonderful. Davia, uh, Princess Leia. I'll need you to stay here. If anyone wakes up, you'll have to keep them subdued. Got it?" Adelaide asked.

"I understand, but what about Obi-wan?"

"We'll find him, and bring him to you. Your duty is to these people," Adelaide tried. "*Your* people."

Princess Leia nodded. "I understand. Be careful, and may the Force be with you."

Adelaide nodded and wondered if the night could get any stranger.

"How will we get there?" Kurt asked again.

"The bikes?" Adelaide suggested. "Darius has one and Davia must, too. If we double, that should be okay. I think." Adelaide escorted Kurt, Sophie, and Darius out to the bikes in the garage. Each of the bikes had a chain with a combination lock securing the front wheel to the frame of the bike. "Dar ... Dick," Adelaide corrected herself, "do you know the combination?"

Darius bent down and studied the lock. "This isn't my bike, I'm afraid. I usually drive us around in my T-Bird. Remember the time we—"

"I'll just stop you there, thanks," Adelaide cut him off. It was, quite literally, as though everyone in one Dizzy

Izzy's costumes had lost their mind.

"Only two vehicular contraptions for four mortals, and they will not go. We need transportation, do we?" Sophie clucked and began to wiggle her fingers. "Night air and shining star, our destination is too far. We have no time for a hike, bring unto me some bikes."

Four shiny black bikes appeared in front of them, each of them held upright by its kickstand.

"That's so rad," Kurt marvelled.

"Thank you," Sophie cooed.

Kurt caught Adelaide's eye. "Do you think we should get the …" Adelaide shook her head before Kurt could finish his sentence, and Kurt breathed a sigh of relief. She knew he was asking about the magic rod they'd taken from a teenager at Rainy Day Games earlier this month. And she knew it was too dangerous. Adelaide was grateful Tetsu was unconscious and couldn't protest.

"Let's do this then," Adelaide said as she climbed onto the bike. She glanced back at the pool house with its sleeping guests, then led her friends down the driveway and toward the town.

Eleven

The even murmur from outside had turned to chaos. There was shouting, hooting, hollering, and the occasional scream. Andy pressed his back against the door.

He had opened it to see what the commotion was and had been rewarded with a giant spider scuttling up the front steps straight toward him. He thought he could still hear it climbing the house, but he did not want to open the door to check.

Andy took a deep breath and wondered what could have caused him to hallucinate.

He was mentally cataloguing everything he had consumed today when the phone rang.

Andy jumped.

"It's the phone you doofus," Andy scolded himself. He glanced at the door, double checked it was locked, and sprinted up the stairs to the kitchen.

"Uh, Katillion residence," Andy said into the receiver.

"Andy? Is that you?" Adelaide's voice came through

the phone. There was a slight note of panic to her voice. Andy's heart skipped a beat.

"Adelaide? Um, hi. It's me. It's Andy."

"Okay, you're okay. Is, um, anything strange going on?" she asked.

"Strange like people are acting nuts out there? Oh yeah." Andy winced as someone dressed as Batman tackled a clown.

"But you're okay?" She sounded concerned.

"Yeah, I'm okay." Andy smiled.

"Just stay inside, all right? We'll try to fix this."

"Fix it how?" Andy asked. "Are you okay?"

"Just stay inside. I have to go."

There was a click and the line went dead.

Andy looked around the house. He jumped as someone banged on the front door. Andy peered out the front window and watched as a zombie shambled toward a person in a white sheet.

"Oh no," Andy said. He ran for the front door, but there was a flash of light.

Andy looked around, disoriented.

He was next to a pay phone, the cold October air biting his cheeks.

A cheerleader, a football player, Albert Einstein,

and a witch stared at him.

"Nice work, Magrathea," Adelaide said to Sophie.

The cheerleader was Adelaide, and she looked even better than Andy had predicted. The outfit was a little bit too big for her, but her long hair was pulled away from her face into a giant ponytail on top of her head.

"Who is *this* guy?" Darius asked.

"Hi, Andy. Thanks for coming," Adelaide said, ignoring Darius. "Not that you had a choice, I suppose. I think we need your help."

Andy looked around. He wasn't sure how he had ended up outside with Adelaide, Darius, Kurt, and his sister, who looked a little too much like a witch now. Then again, he imagined he was far away from the giant spider. Unless he was still hallucinating.

"My help?" Andy asked. "For what exactly?" He wondered briefly where Tetsu was.

"We have to go confront the guy from, I think it's Dizzy Izzy's Costume Emporium. The place your mom got Sophie's costume. The ones that are …" Adelaide trailed off and gestured at Sophie and Darius.

"Go ahead my dear, say what you mean," Sophie cackled. "I fear not everyone here is in their right mind." Sophie eyed Darius with suspicion.

Darius crouched slightly, tensing his muscles as though he were ready to tackle the evil witch.

"See?" Adelaide asked. "Please will you come with us?"

"Of course," Andy said. He looked around at the bikes. They were one short. "How will we …?"

"I'll double with Dick here," Adelaide said with a sigh. She nodded toward Darius. "I'm sure he won't mind."

Andy looked between the two of them.

"Of course, I won't mind, babe. I love it when we're close." Darius eyed Adelaide hungrily.

Andy had a strange urge to step in to tell Darius to stop, or maybe to punch him. Andy wasn't sure, but it made him uncomfortable.

"There is no need to double. That will be too much trouble. If another bike we need, the magic will take heed," Sophie cackled as she wiggled her fingers. Another bike appeared in front of Andy.

He looked between Sophie and Adelaide.

"She's a witch," Adelaide explained. "Magrathea the Magnificent, to be precise. We should get this fixed before your parents pick her up." Adelaide climbed back onto her bike and smiled at Andy. "Your costume is really good."

"Oh, uh, thanks. Um, I really like yours," Andy stuttered. He felt his cheeks blush and hoped it was not as noticeable as it felt.

"All right everyone, on we go," Adelaide said.

They pedaled along the streets and ducked down side roads to avoid trouble. At one point, a group of greasers in a fancy old car started to chase them.

"We haven't time for these guys, it's now time for our bikes to rise," Sophie cackled and wiggled her fingers while she steered her bike with her legs.

All of their bikes started to float off the ground.

"This is like E.T.," Kurt said.

"I can't believe that rhyme worked." Adelaide gripped her handlebars and looked down at the scene below her.

"So, she just says stuff and this happens?" Andy asked.

"Pretty much," Adelaide said. "I think it has to rhyme and she has to wiggle her fingers."

"And focus the magic within me," Magrathea crowed as she turned back toward them. A long smile stretched across her face.

"You missed Princess Leia," Adelaide said to Andy. "And the werewolf."

"I'm okay with that," Andy said.

They continued along for several blocks. People moved this way and that in the streets. They were not as small as ants, but they did look small from the seats of the conjured bikes moving above the buildings in Olympic Vista.

Andy was not sure how Adelaide and Kurt weren't freaking out. And he really did not like the way Darius kept ogling Adelaide.

"There, Soph—Magrathea. Bring us down here," Adelaide directed. "We appreciate your help."

"Of course, she wants to help you. You're the best cheer captain the team has ever seen," Darius called over.

"Wow," Andy said. He hoped he was never as obsessed with anyone as much as Darius seemed to be.

The bikes descended to the ground and Andy and the others clambered off.

The street felt deserted. The door to Dizzy Izzy's Costume Emporium was closed. The lights were off. A handful of costumes still hung in the window of the brick building.

Adelaide leaned her bike against the wall. Kurt followed suit. Andy walked his bike next to Adelaide's. He took her in with her solemn face and her cheer uniform.

A strand of hair had fallen loose from her ponytail. He fought the urge to brush it off her face.

"Hey, I still don't know who you are," Darius said as he stepped forward, "but keep away from my girl."

"Look, I—" Andy started.

"Dick, cut it out," Adelaide said with a sigh. She walked to the door and jiggled the handle. She tried to push the door open, but it would not budge. Adelaide knocked.

They waited, but there was no movement in the store.

Sophie stepped forward. She flexed her fingers as she did so, then she began to wiggle them. "Turn this lock, into a sock!"

Kurt frowned. "That can't—"

The spot in the door where the lock had been was now filled with a white gym sock.

"I don't even understand this," Kurt said, shaking his head. "It totally defies the laws of physics." His big mop of white hair danced back and forth in the light from the streetlamp.

Darius gazed adoringly at Adelaide.

"Thank you," Adelaide said to Sophie. She reached for the doorhandle as Andy opened his mouth to stop her. Then he closed it again. Somehow, she seemed to know what she was doing.

Adelaide eased the door open and stepped inside. Andy shouldered past Darius/Dick to follow close behind.

The floor was dotted with half a dozen empty metal racks. Empty clothing hooks covered most of the walls. The only costumes left were the ones in the window. The counter had a register and a call bell.

"Someone's in my shop," a strange male voice called.

Andy scanned the room, but he could not see whoever it was. He thought the sound had come from the back corner of the store.

"Magrathea, can you make them visible?" Adelaide asked.

"Show yourself you foul beast!" Darius called.

"Tut-tut, that's a temper," the voice called again. It came from near the window this time. "And you are in my shop."

"Whoever caused all this fuss, should now show themselves to us!" Sophie cackled as she wiggled her fingers.

A tall man, taller than Andy thought any man should be, stood next to the window. His face matched the one that had been in the newspaper ads. He wore a suit perfectly tailored to fit his long sinewy body. A long, thin, wicked smile stretched across his sharp face.

"Well, well," Dizzy said. "Quite a treat indeed. Very interesting."

"This is him?" Darius asked.

"Yeah, uh—" Andy started.

Darius roared and charged.

Twelve

Darius, or Dick, as he currently called himself, charged across the costume shop floor.

"Darius!" Adelaide called out.

Dizzy glided out of the way, his shadow a step behind him.

Darius skidded to a stop just before he ran head-first into the wall. He turned, lifted his fist and punched Dizzy in the chest.

Dizzy looked surprised, but uninjured. He took a step back as Darius wound up to take another swing.

"Oh, this is tiresome. Stop," Dizzy commanded.

Darius relaxed. His fist unclenched and his arm dropped to his side.

"That's not good," Kurt murmured.

"Shall we drop the pretense then, hmm?" Dizzy asked. His shadow was where it should be now, but somehow it seemed a different shape than his body.

It was taller and skinnier, and Adelaide was sure it moved separately from him, or perhaps a step out of time.

Adelaide blinked as his appearance changed.

Dizzy's face grew longer, and his limbs longer still. Even his shadow seemed to stretch farther. He was long and wiry, and impossibly inhuman.

"This isn't good," Kurt fretted. "This isn't good at all."

"Easy," Adelaide said slowly. She looked around. Darius stood slack jawed, Kurt was trembling like a leaf, and Andy was inching his way forward to stand between her and Dizzy.

They did not have a lot of options. Sophie looked composed, as she had all evening, and Adelaide wondered if Magrathea's tricks would be a match for Dizzy. A simple rhyme could be all it took.

"Magrathea, can you—"

"None of that." A sinister smile spread across Dizzy's face. His impossibly long fingers drew circles in the air as he turned to look at Sophie. "I know you like to rhyme, my dear, so this one is for you. Witch's nose, witch's hat, take your turn as a big, black cat."

The air around Sophie started to swirl and the long skirt of her costume began to whip this way and that. Everything about her blurred until suddenly she wasn't Sophie, or Magrathea, but a giant black cat. The largest black cat Adelaide had ever seen.

"Is that …? Is that a panther?" Andy stuttered. "Did he turn Sophie into a panther?"

The large black feline shook its head, then opened its mouth and roared. Saliva sprayed from its mouth.

Kurt moaned.

"It's all right, Kurt. I'm right here," Andy said, a slight quaver to his voice.

"Oh, this *is* a fun night now, isn't it? What's your name?" Dizzy asked as he turned to Adelaide.

"My name?" Adelaide asked, confused.

Andy backed away slowly from the panther that had been his sister just moments before.

Dizzy waved his hand and the great beast followed his commands as though this was a circus and he was the ringmaster. The giant cat moved with incredible grace and placed itself between Adelaide and Andy, cutting them off from each other.

It bared its teeth at Andy again.

"Yes, your name, child. Tell me your name." Dizzy moved a step closer and even from across the room, he loomed above of her.

"It's …" Adelaide faltered. She glanced at the panther, at Darius crumpled on the floor.

The edges of Adelaide's mind clouded and she felt compelled to do as Dizzy told her. Her gut told her it was a poor idea. She focused her mind and it felt as if the clouds had parted.

"It's Jessica," Adelaide lied. "It's Jessica, and I know you're responsible for all this." Adelaide gestured at Darius and Sophie. "It's dangerous."

"It's just a bit of fun."

"We don't want this kind of fun. We want it to stop," Kurt moaned.

Dizzy turned as if noticing Kurt for the first time. "An interesting costume to be sure, but it would have been much more fun if it was one of mine. No matter, Kurt. It is Kurt, isn't it? Don't worry your pretty little head about this."

"What does that—"

Before Kurt could finish his sentence, Dizzy pressed the index and middle fingers of one hand against his thumb. Kurt's mouth snapped shut.

"Sleep."

Kurt crumpled to the ground.

"Trick. Or. Treat." Dizzy's smile widened.

"We don't want your tricks," Adelaide said in as firm a voice as she could manage. She forced herself to keep her eyes on Dizzy. "We do *not* want them."

"They're already here," Dizzy said as he moved closer. "And now it's just us three. So, pretty, come here." Dizzy beckoned to her with one finger.

Adelaide forced herself to take a breath. Her palms were sweaty and she was sure this was more trouble than she and her friends, most of whom were incapacitated, had ever faced before. But she was not alone. Andy was still there. Sweet Andy with his mop of golden hair, her boy up the road. She could not allow him to be eaten by a panther that had once been his sister.

"No," she said.

Dizzy looked surprised. "Come here, Jessica," he said again. He beckoned with his finger.

"No. You aren't as powerful as you think," Adelaide said.

Dizzy faltered. He looked between Adelaide and Andy. "My, my, my. Aren't you a perfect pair?"

Adelaide ignored him. "I bet you can't even control what you've done here." She gestured toward the street. "The people who are all dressed up, I bet you don't have as much power as you say. They'll just run about, however they like. Sophie is probably stuck as a cat forever and this"—Adelaide waved her hand around the room—"I suppose you'll just stay here, without another person to sell costumes to. No one will want them now."

"I have control," Dizzy said. He narrowed his eyes at her.

"You can't even make me step toward you," Adelaide mocked.

Dizzy's smile twisted cruelly.

"I bet you can't turn her back," Adelaide said as she pointed at Magrathea.

"I can if I want to," Dizzy retorted. He snapped his fingers and the cat twisted and contorted until Sophie stood there, dressed as a witch with a confused expression. "See?"

"Well, you certainly can't turn him back into how he should be," Adelaide tried as she motioned at Dick/Darius who still stood slack jawed.

"Child's play!" Dizzy scoffed. He snapped his fingers and Darius blinked.

Adelaide was sure it was Darius, not Dick, and she raised a finger to her lips as he opened his mouth to speak. She knew he would say her name, and one look at Kurt told her that would be a bad idea.

"Well, there is no way you could undo what you've done. Not even if you wanted to. I suspect Magrathea could, but I'm guessing you created a witch more powerful than you are," Adelaide taunted.

She caught Andy's eyes. He looked at her, horrified.

"You pathetic, underestimating little *worm*!" Dizzy bellowed. He stretched taller still until it was as if the whole building itself had stretched to make space for him.

Adelaide refused to avert her gaze, though her knees trembled and her palms dripped with sweat.

"I am the most powerful creature you've ever met," Dizzy boomed.

"Prove it. I'll only believe you're as powerful as you say, if you can prove it. Make all of those people"—Adelaide gestured outside the shop—"forget tonight happened. Undo it," Adelaide demanded.

The room around them started to swirl.

Adelaide closed her eyes. She felt the pizza rising in her stomach.

Thirteen

Andy looked around. He was on the landing just inside the front door of his house. He was still dressed in his James Bond costume and in one hand he held a bowl of candy.

He was alone.

The kitchen phone rang.

Andy ran up the steps, tripping on his own feet.

"Hello? Hello?" he called into the receiver.

"Andy? Hi, it's me." Adelaide's voice came through the phone line. "I wanted to make sure you were okay. Do you remember it?"

"I remember it." Andy looked around, confused by how he'd arrived back in the house. "Are you all right?"

"Me? Oh, I'm fine. I can take care of myself. Hey, um … thanks, Andy. I have to go."

"Oh, uh, sure. Yeah. Night."

There was a click as the call was disconnected.

Andy set the receiver back in the hook and looked around.

"Katillion. Andy Katillion," he said with a smile.

***

Darius scanned the room and saw Adelaide by the phone. The clock read 10:48. He was not sure where the night had disappeared to. He made his way over to her.

Kurt scurried through the crowd and grabbed Adelaide's arm.

"Please tell me you remember that," Kurt begged.

"I remember, Kurt. It's okay. It's over." Adelaide patted his hand. "I'm not sure how we got back here, but I think everything is all right now."

"How we got back here?" Darius asked, confused. "I, um, think I have to apologize, but I don't know what for," Darius said. He had vague recollections of professing his love, but much of the evening was a hazy blur.

Kurt laughed.

Adelaide smiled.

"You weren't yourself," Adelaide assured him. "Though, I have to ask, do you think you'll play football, like, ever?"

"I think I just dreamed I did," Darius said with a frown. He searched his memory but it was as though he was trying to catch water with a sieve. "I don't think I liked football-player me."

"None of us did," Kurt said as he patted Darius' shoulder.

Tetsu and Sophie walked toward them.

"I feel like I haven't seen you most of the night," Tetsu said to Adelaide.

"Too busy with soda and pizza, I suspect," Adelaide teased. "Oh, shoot. My mom," Adelaide said. "I'll talk to you in a minute, Darius."

"Oh, sure." Darius turned to the others. "This party…something happened, didn't it?"

Tetsu looked between Kurt and Darius, confused.

Kurt just smiled and shook his head.

***

It was a quiet drive home. Adelaide suspected her mother could vaguely recall some of the evening's details, like a bad dream she couldn't quite shake.

In the end there had not been any injuries. Some of her classmates were slightly dazed, but all in all, people seemed to have forgotten the event.

Adelaide looked out the window at the Katillion

house as they passed it. There was a dim light in the living room window. The dining room light, she thought. She wondered if Andy was still up. The house faded from view as Belinda drove past the last few houses and parked the car in their driveway.

"Thanks again, Mama," Adelaide said as she unbuckled her seatbelt.

"Anything for you, baby," Belinda answered.

Adelaide smiled at her mother.

The two of them climbed out of the K-car, walked up the front steps and entered the house.

"I'm going to bed. Have a good sleep," Adelaide said. She leaned up and kissed her mother on her cheek.

"Night, baby," Belinda said. She kissed the top of Adelaide's head.

Adelaide climbed the wooden staircase and went into her room. Her curtains were already drawn, and she suspected her mother had closed them while she was at the Belcouer's. Belinda had been trying hard to act like a parent over the last few weeks. Adelaide pulled out her pajamas from under her pillow and got changed. She couldn't believe her trick on Dizzy had worked.

There was a scratch at her window. Adelaide frowned and stepped toward it. She grasped one of the curtains, pulled it back and peered through the glass. The light from her room reflected on the window, revealing only a reflection of her and not what was on the other side. She squinted and stepped forward.

Two green eyes looked back at her.

Adelaide's breath caught in her throat.

A calico cat reached up a paw and scratched at the window.

Adelaide exhaled and stepped forward. She let the curtain fall behind her as she slid her window up and open.

"Well, who are you?" Adelaide asked the unfamiliar cat. She looked past him into the yard, but it was empty.

"Never mind that," the cat said. Adelaide started. "You'll need to watch your back now. He'll be mad at you for that. He'll come for revenge when you least expect it. He always does. Always."

The cat turned and padded down the roof. When he reached the gutter, he leapt off the roof, away from the house.

Adelaide blinked in disbelief as the calico cat flew through the night air toward the woods.

***

Andy set his bike against the brick storefront. Adelaide set hers next to his.

"You're sure about this?" he asked.

"I am. Thanks for coming. It would probably be stupid to come alone," Adelaide said.

The door to the shop was wide open and a few costumes still hung in the window.

Andy walked into the store and Adelaide followed.

A few stray leaves had blown in with the wind.

"You know, I wouldn't win games to prove my love to anyone. I'd just show them." Andy flushed as soon as the words were out of his mouth. He could not bear to look at Adelaide.

A piece of paper on the floor next to one of the metal racks caught his eye. Andy walked forward and picked it up.

It was a painting of a tall, thin man that resembled a mix of the two figures he had seen in the shop last night. The material was thicker than paper, more like cardstock. The figure held a single wand and, below the image, were three words: *The Dizzy Prince*.

Adelaide sighed as she peered over his shoulder. "That's probably not good. I guess the cat was right."

"I don't think we can do anything about it now,"

Andy said.

"I suppose not."

"Why do you think he couldn't affect you?" Andy asked. He had been impressed at how well Adelaide had held her ground last night and had not stopped thinking about it. "Sophie and Darius were wearing his costumes, but this Dizzy fellow, he put Kurt to sleep as well. Kurt made that costume, didn't he?"

"Yes, he did. It was Kurt's name, I think. Sophie and Darius were in his costumes, but he learned Kurt's name."

"Oh." Andy hadn't thought of that, and he blushed at how obvious it was. Then he blushed deeper as he recalled using Kurt's name. "How'd you know to not use your real name?"

"I guessed. Names hold power. I heard that once. I don't remember where." She paused. "It's okay, you know. We all make mistakes. And Kurt's fine now."

Andy breathed a sigh of relief. "Do you want to get out of here? We could, um, we could go for a bike ride?" he asked hopefully.

"I'd like that."

"Me, too." Andy smiled and fought the impulse to reach for Adelaide's hand. "So, is this the kind of thing you guys do?"

"Sometimes," Adelaide admitted. "That's weird, right?" She glanced around the shop one last time, then turned and headed for the door.

Andy followed her. "No, I think it's mint. Thanks again for including me." Andy flinched as his voice raised an octave. "You can, um, you can call me again." He looked down at the ground. "If you want," he added. Andy glanced over at Adelaide who had paused.

"Yeah?" she asked, studying him.

"Yeah."

"I might just do that," Adelaide said as she continued walking.

Andy kept pace with her as they collected their bikes. "I'd really like that." Andy recalled Dizzy's comment: *Aren't you two the perfect pair.* He wasn't sure what Dizzy had meant, but he liked the idea of being a pair with Adelaide.

Acknowledgements

Many thanks to: Darren, Bonnie, Mike,
Ken, Carly, and Darcy.
And to Emily Holden, who went above and beyond.

About the Olympic Vista Chronicles

Everything twelve-year-old Adelaide Winter knows about her Washington state hometown is turned on its head when Darius Belcouer moves to Olympic Vista at the end of summer 1986.

The two become fast friends as they bond over the mystery of a local haunted house Darius wants to explore. The house, it turns out, is only the tip of the iceberg. They quickly discover the more they dig, the more they uncover, and the trail leads back to The Link, a research and development facility in town. Together, Adelaide and her friends delve into the strange occurrences around Olympic Vista.

A tale of friendship, horror, and coming of age in the late 80s.

Yesterday's Gone (Book One)
Songs from the Wood (Book Two)
Costumes & Copiers (Book Three)

About the Author

Kelly Pawlik dabbled with story writing from a young age. She spent her childhood reading, dressing her beloved cat, Midnight, up in doll clothes, and hunting garter snakes in the backyard. Her childhood dream was to be an author and she is proud to be bringing character to life with her Olympic Vista Chronicles novellas.

Kelly is a tabletop roleplaying game (TTRPG) writer and has released multiple RPG supplements with her husband under their micro-publishing company, Dire

Rugrat Publishing. She has also contributed to several best-selling works with Kobold Press.

Kelly lives on Vancouver Island, BC with her husband, their three inquisitive children, and two lazy cats.

You can follow Kelly on:

Facebook: kellypawlikauthor
Instagram: kellypawlikauthor
Twitter: @KellyPawlik84

Sign up to receive Kelly's newsletter and you'll get access to sneak peeks of upcoming novellas, behind the scenes information and other exclusive content including bonus scenes and short stories.

Visit her website at olympicvistapublishing.com for more information.

Manufactured by Amazon.ca
Bolton, ON